NIGH...

The first Apache appeared like a ghost, emerging soundlessly from the night, stealing silently across the open ground to the corral. He stopped to scout around. Moonlight touched his face a moment before he slipped under the bottom rail.

The horses whinnied softly and bunched at the far side of the corral. There had to be at least one more Apache nearby, Brandish was certain, but he could not detect him immediately, and he knew he would never spot the Indian until the warrior made a move. By then it would be too late. The horses would be gone, and with them any hope for escape.

The Apache in the corral had his back to him. Brandish took the opportunity to slip out of cover. In an instant he was under the bottom rail. The nervous sounds of the horses covered his footsteps until he was almost upon him…

Other *Leisure* Westerns by Douglas Hirt:
McKENDREE

BRANDISH

DOUGLAS HIRT

LEISURE BOOKS   NEW YORK CITY

To Alice Carter

A LEISURE BOOK®

November 1997

Published by

Dorchester Publishing Co., Inc.
276 Fifth Avenue
New York, NY 10001

If you purchased this book without a cover you should be aware that this book is stolen property. It was reported as "unsold and destroyed" to the publisher and neither the author nor the publisher has received any payment for this "stripped book."

Copyright © 1997 by Douglas Hirt

All rights reserved. No part of this book may be reproduced or transmitted in any form or by any electronic or mechanical means, including photocopying, recording or by any information storage and retrieval system, without the written permission of the Publisher, except where permitted by law.

ISBN 0-8439-4323-8

The name "Leisure Books" and the stylized "L" with design are trademarks of Dorchester Publishing Co., Inc.

Printed in the United States of America.

BRANDISH

Chapter One

Ethan Brandish emerged from the broken tableland at the rim of an ancient lava flow and reined his horse to a stop. For a long, watchful moment he remained motionless against the silent tilting slabs of rock that rose up around him. Only the distant *kya-kya-kya* of an eagle circling high overhead disturbed the hot, still air.

Behind him a ragged background confused the skyline. Ahead, the trail descended the side of the escarpment to a wide, sunbaked plain of Sulphur Spring Valley below. In the distance, when he squinted hard against the shimmering land that lay before him, Brandish could just barely discern a faint ribbon of green that marked the passage of water. Somewhere along that stream was a stout roof to sleep under, and a plate of something good to eat. Guaranteed.

Brandish found himself grinning as he studied the widening plain below with the careful eye of a seasoned tactician while his horse cooled in the shade of a finger of rock pointing skyward.

The dust of the last two days, mingled with his own sweat, had colored the faded blue of his uniform blouse and trousers to the same dull red-brown of the surrounding land. The shadow of a new beard darkened his cheeks. All in all, by Ethan Brandish's reckoning, he blended in quite satisfactorily.

"Quite satisfactorily, indeed," he said aloud, giving the impatient roan a quieting pat on the neck. The horse shifted under the weight of its rider, its muscles flinched and rolled beneath the McClellan saddle. A crack, like a rifle shot, from his horse's impatient hoof upon hard rock told Brandish the animal was ready to continue. Brandish took a long drink from his canteen and twisted the stopper back in place, seating it tightly with a slap of his palm.

Yes, he would be difficult to see against the backdrop of this hellish land, but years of dealing with the Apaches impelled Ethan Brandish to keep a sharp eye out just the same. He frowned as he recalled the dispatch from Fort Bowie that had come across his desk the day before he had left. It had been signed in Lieutenant Colonel George Crook's own hand, and that was not something to take frivolously.

Brandish rested a while longer in the bit of shade he had found, then he nudged his horse onto the narrow trail, allowing the animal to pick

Brandish

its way off the caprock at its own pace. Except for the scrape of iron shoes against rock, and the occasional rattle of the saber strapped to the back of his saddle whenever the black wall of lava rock pressed too near to the ledge, a stifling, invasive quietness enveloped the hot afternoon. No animal with any sense ventured out until evening brought coolness to this land. No, only traveling ex–cavalry officers, he mused . . . and the Apaches.

Narrowed against the afternoon glare, Brandish's brown eyes searched the vastness of the plain below. To the northwest, the Galiuro Mountains stood indistinct against the hazy blue sky. The green ribbon in the distance meandered back toward those mountains and disappeared beneath the rising waves of heat; its headwaters were up there somewhere, he knew.

A tactical feature to keep in mind, Brandish thought, and then he grinned tightly to himself. *A tactical feature that would serve me little use now.* But old habits tend to die a slow and sometimes painful death. The topography of the land was less a concern than Crook's dispatch. . . .

He had read it in the stark afternoon light coming through headquarters' windows at Fort Lowell. Afterward, he had flung it onto his newly cleaned desk, sending a mild curse after it.

Across the small office, with his hands clasped behind his back, Sergeant McGrath had turned from the window and lowered a bushy eyebrow at him.

"Trouble, sir?"

Brandish had squinted into the harsh sunlight that framed his first sergeant. The glare washed out McGrath's features and set his brilliant crown of red hair blazing like a band of coals beneath a smithy's bellows.

"Yellow Shirt again," Brandish said, leaning back in the desk chair.

McGrath glanced at the dispatch upon the desk. "I thought we put an end to that bit of trouble last winter."

"So, apparently, did Crook." Brandish pulled thoughtfully at the long, twisted end of his mustache. "Apparently Yellow Shirt and some of his warriors escaped back up into the Tonto Basin. While Crook was negotiating with the bands to move them onto the reservation at Camp Verde, Yellow Shirt was regrouping, and recruiting more braves."

McGrath frowned. "Now you just put them 'paches out of mind, sir," he said. "It ain't none of your concern no more, Captain. Why, after tomorrow's bugle call you'll no longer be part of this here man's army, nosiree! You'll be a civilian, and that Yellow Shirt fellow will be the problem of the colonel, and that new captain, Benton Ross."

Brandish grunted and tried not to let his displeasure show. "Ross is green as a willow sapling, you know that. Besides, he's a political appointee. Thinks he can move out here and round up renegades like they were a bunch of truant schoolchildren." He plucked two cigars from the

Brandish

humidor on his desk and handed one to McGrath.

McGrath grinned and shrugged his meaty shoulders as he bit off the end and leaned into Brandish's match. "I guess I know all about them gover'ment appointees. Served a while with Carrington at Fort Phil Kearny."

Both men chuckled.

McGrath went on, "He'll learn right soon enough, Captain. The colonel put me in charge of teaching him the way of things out here."

"Hmmm. Well, in that case, extend my condolences to the unfortunate Captain Ross," Brandish replied stoically.

McGrath chuckled. "I sort of reckon he ain't had much practical Indian experience, what with him comin' straight from division headquarters in San Francisco."

"San Francisco, for God's sakes." Brandish snatched up Crook's dispatch off the desktop and put it on top of the neat pile of papers at the corner. He'd gone through all the paperwork that morning, placing the dispatches and notes that the new captain would need to see here, on the desk, and filing the rest—for the first and last time in his three years at post headquarters—in the filing cabinets. For the most part, those cabinets had held only his revolver and holster, some ammunition, and a dusty bottle of whiskey that he had passed around three weeks ago when his discharge papers had come through.

"Why the hell do they pick raw paper pushers

for this post?" Brandish said as if speaking to himself.

"Probably a screwup, Captain, don't you know? We always get the ones who have stepped on official toes one time or another back East, or don't know which end the bit goes in. Ross strikes me as one of 'em, Captain."

It was true. Brandish felt a surge of irritation. The isolated outposts seemed to be filled with more than their fair share of men who had failed elsewhere. But he knew that was not the case as far as Captain Benton Ross was concerned. Brandish had never met his replacement, but reputations spread easily through the Regular Army. Benton Ross's father had been a brevet major general during the war, and afterward he had secured an appointment to West Point for his son, Benton. But Benton Ross had none of his father's qualities, and shortly after graduation found himself assigned to Schofield's San Francisco headquarters—safely shuffling papers, far from the dangers on the frontier. Not a place to gain rank, especially since congress had recently cut in half the size of the army.

The word among the officers was that Benton was an ambitious man, using his father's influence to acquire an appointment on the line. And although congress was no longer handing out brevets, service under fire was still the fastest way for a young officer to gain rank.

Well, Captain Ross, you are certainly coming to the right place for that.

Brandish frowned, glanced at the dispatch

folded neatly on the stack with all the others, and said, "I don't like this. I feel like I'm handing over the reins of a stampeding team and about to jump off before the whole damned cart heads over the edge."

"Now, Captain, it ain't like that at all," McGrath said. "I'll see to it that Ross don't make no damned fool mistakes right off, and after a few months Captain Ross will be sharp as the rest of us." McGrath cleared his throat and added, "Of course, he ain't never gonna fill your boots, Captain."

Brandish glanced up and grinned. "Always the diplomat, McGrath. You'll go far in the cavalry."

"Captain," McGrath said, wounded, "it be the very truth, the saints be my witness! You know I don't lick no man's boots." His eyebrows came together and he shifted to a different matter. "You know, Captain, I've been thinking 'bout you riding off on the morrow. There's a patrol heading out to Fort Bowie next week. What with Yellow Shirt on the prowl, maybe you'd like to stick around and ride under escort."

"And steal the fire from under Benton Ross's first command? No, thanks, Sergeant. Besides, I promised Frank and Ruby Cohen I'd swing by the stage stop and see them before I left the territory. Afterward I'll take the old Overland Stage road over to Fort Bowie and give Crook my farewell. Tell you what, Sergeant, we'll have a farewell drink too, you and me, when your patrol comes in to Fort Bowie."

McGrath grinned, but failed to hide the worry

that came to his blue eyes, and Brandish could see no reason to go into further detail as to what Crook's dispatch had said. McGrath was already weighing the possibilities.

"That's dangerous territory to be riding about in alone, Captain."

"That it is, Sergeant," Brandish said, pushing back his chair as he stood. "But Cochise has made peace and there are only a few like Yellow Shirt left to bring in. I'll be all right."

Brandish was a lean man, hardened by the rigors of the Arizona frontier. He stood over the sergeant by four inches—almost too tall for a horse soldier—but that never stopped Ethan Brandish from pursuing a command. Now, at forty-two, he was giving it all up. And for what? He didn't know exactly, except that there had to be something else out there, something other than rattlesnakes, mesquite, and the Apaches.

The Apaches! Mesquite and rattlesnakes he could easily do without, but the Apaches—? Something had changed there. These last few years Ethan Brandish had grown to respect his savage opponent. By way of the Apache scouts that Crook had enlisted into the Regulars, Brandish had developed a growing understanding of these Indians—the way they thought, the way they believed. In battle, Ethan Brandish had been forced to admire their courage and fierceness, and he resented having to hunt them down, round them up like cattle, and drive them into reservation life. Yet he saw no way to help them either. Perhaps that was why he was giving up

Brandish

his commission, a pension, and a life, although demanding, most rewarding too.

"McGrath, tomorrow the colonel will give me a five-rifle salute to remember old wounds by." Brandish looked around the adobe walls of his spanking new office, at the sparse furniture, the filing cabinets, at the wall map of the Territory. Camp Lowell had become Fort Lowell only a few months earlier, with new buildings, a new location, and soon a new regiment. Word was, the 8th was about to replace the battle-weary 23rd Infantry.

Brandish put aside the somber thought and grinned at McGrath. "What do you say we march on over to the canteen and celebrate with a bottle of bourbon?"

McGrath's eyes widened like a Kansas prairie. "Captain, you know I'd follow you into Yellow Shirt's very own stronghold if you asked," he said, coming vaguely to attention.

Brandish winked and said, "Especially if there happened to be a bottle of whiskey waiting for you when you got there."

Brandish recalled with a pang of regret that last trip across the parade ground to the canteen with his first sergeant. Perhaps his future would amount to no more than reliving past glories, but wasn't that the real reason for his early retirement? Here he was, barely into his forties, with a good many years still ahead of him. Ethan Brandish, captain, retired, had no intention of spending the rest of them fighting Indians.

Brandish reined to a halt on the steep trail and scanned the wide plain below. Nothing stirred out on the short, brown grass. No distant band of roving Indians. Not even the ever-present pronghorn were moving about in this heat. Perhaps he was being overly cautious. With more than a thousand square miles to roam, chances were slight that he would cross paths with Yellow Shirt.

His eyes fixed upon a distant speck on the harsh plain. He raised his field glasses. Still far to the east, sitting among the green of the waterway, the faint lines of corrals and scattering of buildings marked it plainly. The old stage stop.

An hour's ride brought him into the cool shade of cottonwood and oak trees that lined the creek. Brandish brought his horse to water, washed his face, and soaked his hat. He glanced around at the mesquite and blue sage that seemed to stretch on forever. The mountains to the northwest had lowered on the horizon, where the haze of hot air obscured all but a hint of their uneven peaks. He looked to the southeast, more or less the same direction the creek flowed. The stage stop was no more than another hour's ride now. The sun would be on its way down by then, and Ruby Cohen would be preparing dinner for the travelers the now infrequent stage runs would have brought—if they'd brought any at all. Brandish's grin hitched up. Well, Ruby would have at least one guest tonight.

He stuck his foot into the stirrup then changed his mind and unslung his canteen. Old habits do

Brandish

die hard, he chided himself, kneeling once again by the water's edge to top it off.

"Too many years in this dry country," he said softly, and grinned as he stepped up into the saddle. "A man begins to talk to himself if he doesn't watch it."

The horse, taking advantage of the shade where it could be found, plodded on alongside the trickle of water with the sun, lowering at Brandish's back, glinting off the pommel of his saber buckled to the back of his saddle.

As he rode along, Brandish played a soldier's game of calculating distances. The line of the Dragoon Mountains to the west he had just descended, perhaps six miles off now. The Chiricahua Mountains farther east, maybe thirty miles. The stage stop ahead, no more than two or three. He allowed the conscious part of his mind to roam freely while another part, separate in a way he never quite understood, stayed alert, reading and evaluating signs along the way.

His thoughts touched briefly on the fort he had left behind, and lingered a bit on Sergeant McGrath. A twinge momentarily drew his lips into a frown. This trip was taking him forever away from a life that had been so much a part of him for over twenty years.

Ahead was a new life waiting for him.

But what would he do in a civilian world?

Before Ethan Brandish could answer that, a warning exploded within his brain and brought him instantly out of his reverie. He reined to a stop, turned the horse back a few paces, and swung off his saddle to the ground. In the earth by the water's edge he knelt and placed a finger into an indentation. All along the stream's bank the soft ground was pocked with the hoofprints of a great number of animals, mostly unshod ponies, but among them were some that had worn iron shoes.

The hair slowly lifted off his neck. A large band of Indians had paused here to water their horses. The footprints of men mingled with those of the animals. They had passed here not long ago, he calculated by the sharp edges of the prints. Where the hooves had splashed water up onto the bank, the mud had dried and cracked. Twenty-four hours . . . perhaps a little less. He ran a hand over the coarse growth at his chin and looked west, the direction the riders had taken.

There might have been a dozen good reasons for their presence here, and even a few to account for the shod horses and mules he discovered among the tracks of the Indian ponies, but Brandish had spent too many years dealing with the Apaches to believe anything but the worse.

A sudden urgency now impelled him as he climbed back onto his horse and removed the Springfield carbine from the saddle scabbard. He broke open the action, checked the round in the chamber, and snapped the breech closed again, settling the rifle in the crook of his arm.

As he urged his horse forward, his fingers tightened around the Springfield, draining with each flex a little of the tension that had suddenly drawn the dusty blue blouse taut across his back.

Brandish

He blinked over his shoulder at the lowering sun, then ahead to where the stage stop lay.

To his left he heard only the whisper of flowing water, and to his right he heard nothing at all.

Chapter Two

When the first broken outlines of the stage stop appeared through the stand of cottonwood and live oaks, Ethan Brandish reined over and splashed across the shallow stream, coming up behind the blacksmith's hut, where a small corral was built up against a rise of land. A side door hung open.

Brandish urged his horse toward it to have a look inside, but the wide, double doors in the front of the building had been closed and barred, and only a faint, dusty light filtered through the cracks and through the shuttered windows. He dismounted and stuck his head in the open side doorway, and instantly pulled back. The sickly sweet odor of death was heavy and filled the hot, stagnant air.

Brandish tried to shove the door wider, but a

pair of legs stretched out on the floor beyond impeded its movement. He stepped over them and slipped through the narrow gap. In the hazy light he saw the dark lump of a body sprawled there.

It was Ralph Tabadore.

Brandish frowned. He did not know this man well. They had only met and spoken a time or two in the past when he had stopped by the stage stop to pay his regards to Ruby and Frank. Tabadore had been a powerfully built man in life, and in death his stiff fingers still clutched the handle of a heavy hammer, where bits of hair and dried blood clung.

Flies were already swarming the body. *Opportunistic beasts*.

A weight seemed to descend upon Brandish, pressing his spirit as he retreated from the rancid air and slipped back outside. He made a quick survey of the area and his view settled on the adobe stage stop a few dozen paces away. Out back of it were the corrals, a long barn for the mules the stage line used, and a second, smaller barn for hay and feed.

Brandish drew the heavy hammer of his rifle back to full cock as he strode around the front of the main building where the faded letters on a placard hanging above the porch reflected a bygone era: BUTTERFIELD OVERLAND MAIL COMPANY.

Below the placard hung a second, smaller sign, its paint fresh and bright in comparison: COHEN STAGE STOP.

The Butterfield line had closed down its southern line back in '61, when Confederate soldiers had advanced into the Territory, but Ruby and Frank Cohen had stayed on just the same, keeping the place going despite hard times, the War of the Rebellion, and the Apaches. It served as an unofficial mail station for the scattered settlers, catering to the occasional traveler, and the slightly more frequent coaches of the Frederick Mercantile Passenger Service Company.

And the FMPS Company had, unfortunately, made a stop this time. The company's newly repainted Celerity coach, one which the Butterfield Company had sold off after their final demise in '69, lay overturned in the front yard like a giant black and red beetle. Someone had taken great care to polish its red-painted trim and wheel spokes, and if it hadn't been for the arrows that splintered its wood and cracked its shiny lacquer coat, Brandish might have seen his reflection in the black panels.

But now more than a dozen bullet holes riddled the coach, its canvas top was slashed, its leather luggage boot ripped open like the belly of a gutted animal—and its bowels strewn about. Traveling trunks split open upon hitting the ground had spilled their contents, and carpetbags disgorged their belongings. Paper and clothing were scattered about. Some unidentifiable pieces of iron, like the drill bits that hard rock miners used, lay nearby. Fragments of a white and red checked cloth had been carried by the wind to the pond, and more of the same material was twisted into the dry brush that clung to a two-strand barbed wire fence along the yard's eastern edge. There were no mules about. The Apaches would have taken those away.

He turned toward the station and came to a halt. The grim lines of his face pulled deeper at the corners of his mouth. A short, bald-headed man lay at the foot of the porch. Another man, younger, was up on the porch with an arrow through his neck. Brandish took a firmer grip on the Springfield rifle and stepped under the swinging, faded Butterfield shingle.

The clay olla that hung in the shade of the porch had escaped the battle with its dipper still in place. Just inside the doorway, Brandish came up short and a tightness gripped his throat and squeezed down like a fist.

Ruby and Frank Cohen were sprawled at his feet in the unnatural contortions of violent death.

The stench of death that he knew so well fouled the hot air. In the corner, a scorched stain marked the wall where a fire had been attempted and failed, and the charred remains of a wooden cabinet lay among the ashes on the hard, adobe mud floor.

Broken glass crunched beneath Brandish's boots. He ducked under a low doorway into a darkened back room where Frank and Ruby's bedding was spread across the floor. The drawers of a bureau had been yanked out and rifled. Both front and rear windows had been shuttered and barred in a hasty, but futile attempt to keep this undefended portion of the building secure.

The grim line of his lips compressed further. He lifted one of the heavy crossbars and pulled the thick pine shutters open, wrenching out an arrow that got in the way. Part of the curtain had been caught between the panels in someone's haste to close it, and it came free now as they swung apart. More bullet holes pocked the outside of them, but not surprisingly, none had penetrated completely through.

A breeze teased the ends of Ruby's white curtains. A dusty shaft of late-afternoon light fell upon the disheveled bed as evening approached.

Brandish studied the lay of the land beyond the open window; his soldier's eye measuring the defensibility of the place, and the probable direction of the first attack. He frowned. It had been an ill-conceived location for a stage stop. The rising land no more than seventy-five yards beyond the barns was too convenient a place to stage an attack from. But there was good water here, and a natural pond which probably figured into the locating of the station.

The two barns out back had been constructed between the station and the rising land, further enhancing the cover for the Apaches. In the dusty patch of ground between the barns and station, Brandish saw the sixth body . . . and a dog.

Brandish climbed out over the windowsill and straightened up behind the building. He'd seen death before, but here, with only the lonely scolding of a raven perched atop the corner of the farthest barn to disturb the silence of it, he knew a deeper sadness. Those other times, in battle, it had been the dirtier side of an otherwise dirty job. This was somehow different. Ethan Brandish was no longer in command of troops. He was a civilian, in a civilian world.

Why should that make a difference now?

Warily, Brandish moved away from the cover of the building and crossed the open yard to where the man and dog lay. The dog was a collie—or, at least it was collielike. Most probably a mutt. It was pinned to the ground by an Apache war lance, its golden fur streaked by an ugly black crust of dried blood.

Brandish scanned the hills, and probed the shadows alongside the barns, turning a sweeping view to the flat, endless land that marched out in front of the stage stop. Still nothing moved out there. Over by the blacksmith's hut, his horse had its head down in a patch of dried grass.

Something was wrong here. Something that went beyond all the death. His forehead creased, but whatever it was that troubled him was yet too subtle to get hold of. Still, he was sure it would come to him eventually.

He knelt by the man, a big black man who had taken an arrow in the spine and three bullets before the Apaches had been able to put him down. Like the blacksmith, he had been a powerful man, with strong shoulders and thick arms. Beneath the body was a furrow cut in the hard ground, as if something had been removed from his dead fingers and dragged out from under him.

The black man's right hand was balled into a rock-hard fist. Brandish pried the stiff fingers apart and three .44 rimfire cartridges fell to the ground. Spread on the dusty land around him were a dozen more spent shells. It did not take much imagination to piece together a pretty clear picture of this man's last few minutes of life. With a Winchester repeating rifle blazing away, this man had managed to keep the Indians at bay. How many did he take with him? Perhaps each shot met its mark, but Brandish suspected that more likely only five or six fell before the hammer finally clicked on an empty chamber. Then he'd had to pause to pump fresh ammunition into the weapon. Perhaps it was at this point the arrow had struck, or one of the bullets. In any event, the black man had died, and afterward, the Indians had dragged the prized weapon from under him.

Well, it made for interesting speculation. Brandish glanced over at the dog. The dog's story could never be pieced together, but he would have liked to think it had died protecting its slain master.

Speculation. That was all it was—all it could ever be now.

Brandish briefly ran his fingers through the dog's thick, golden fur and stood to further survey the yard.

What had prompted the attack? The long, empty corrals shook a silent, accusing finger. It had been for the mules and horses, and more. . . .

The Cohens had never had trouble when Cochise led the Chiricahuas. But Yellow Shirt was not Chiricahua. He was Coyotero, a White Mountain Apache, and his bitterness at Cochise's surrender was great—almost as great as his hatred for the white intruders in this harsh land that the Apaches called home.

Ethan Brandish shrugged off the gloom that had closed in around him and tugged speculatively at the end of his mustache. The open ground that stretched away from the stage stop held no more bodies. The Indians had removed all of their own dead. He glanced back at the dead black man and again was struck with that uneasy feeling that he was overlooking something here. Something important.

Suddenly Ethan Brandish knew what it was. They all still had their hair—the blacksmith, the two out front, Frank and Ruby Cohen, and this man with his shaggy mane that hung to his shoulders. The Apaches had left without taking scalps!

Brandish recalled that something like this had happened once before . . . in '68 at the Battle of Many Hills. It had been Comanches, not Apaches that time. They had ambushed and overpowered a dozen troops in a narrow pass there, had killed all but two men, when suddenly they had left the battle in strength, and in an hurry—not bothering to take scalps, and the reason why was . . .

Movement caught the corner of his eye. Inside the barn a shadow had shifted where the low afternoon sun slanted through a small glassless window. Brandish's fist tightened around the Springfield carbine and he leaped toward the corrals, rolling under a pole railing and flattening himself against the unplastered adobe wall of the barn. A door hung open in the gathering shadows. Brandish slid up alongside it, and as he listened, he could pick out the rustling sounds of something moving around inside the barn.

He paused, heart pounding. Crouching, he turned into the doorway and dropped to his haunches within the narrow space of an empty stall. The odor of hay and manure swelled in the still air. He waited, barely breathing, listening to his heart thumping like a parade-ground drum as his eyes grew accustomed to the dim light.

Out of the stillness came the splash of water, followed by a trickling sound as if someone were wringing out a wet rag. Then a woman's voice whispered low—too low for Brandish to make out her words.

He moved forward, his rifle ready, stepped out into the gallery between the horse stalls, and made his way silently through the barn, coming to a soundless halt at one of the stalls. The shadows were deep here, with only a fading shaft of sunlight through the window striking the adobe wall beyond them.

Her back was toward him, hunched forward as she bent over the body of a man there on the dirt floor. Through the angle of her outstretched arm, Brandish saw the shaft of an arrow protruding from the man's left side, just below his ribs, rising and dropping with each shallow breath.

The woman carefully adjusted the damp cloth that she had spread over the man's fevered forehead, her fingers touching it gently, almost tim-

Brandish

idly, as if fearing to do any more harm to him.

"Oh, Jonathan," came her plaintive whisper as she placed a palm gently upon the cloth, as if to test the coolness of it.

Ethan advanced a step into the stall and was about to speak when the woman suddenly became aware of his presence. In a startled instant she saw him there, and like a frightened animal she leaped for a cocked Winchester leaning against the wall.

Through the gloom of the dusty light Brandish saw the blind panic in her face as she clutched up the rifle, her eyes wide and ablaze with the fire of hatred as she wheeled toward him.

The rifle in her hands came up at him, and in the tight confines of the horse stall, its roar was deafening. . . .

Chapter Three

More than half his lifetime had been lived honing the reflexes necessary to survive on the Western frontier. It had been a gradual process, begun in his freewheeling youth, cut loose of apron strings at age twelve. Later, survival was a lesson well learned as a green private in the Federal Army. Three years at West Point had taught him the more esoteric skills of survival, and then the guns at Fort Sumter boomed one fateful day in April of '61, and the war that followed brought all the remaining rough edges down to a fine cutting line.

By the time Ethan Brandish had graduated from that campaign, a fresh lieutenant, fighting neighbors and kinsmen had left a bitter taste, a taste best washed clean by the wide open Western lands. When President Johnson signed the act to reorganize the army in '66, Brandish accepted a position at Fort Buford in the Dakota Territory, and with it a promotion to captain in the United States Cavalry.

He moved on from there to command a company at Fort Reno, and then another down at Fort Garland, in the newly organized territory of Colorado, working his way always south, where the winters were tolerable, and the summers hellish, finally transferring in the spring of '69 to Schofield's Division of the Pacific, to fight the Apaches in Arizona.

Those years had stropped the edge of his instincts until now, with this wild-eyed woman swinging the rifle around toward him, Ethan Brandish did not need to pause and think what to do next.

He was instantly in motion.

Her frantic eyes told him all he needed to know. She wasn't seeing him, a white man and apparently a cavalry officer, since he still wore his uniform. She was seeing the Apaches again, and in that moment he understood the horrible scar the attack on the stage stop had left upon her.

Brandish flung himself beneath the rifle barrel as the weapon barked and spit flame in the dimness of the horse stall. The bullet splintered the pole railing where an instant before he'd been standing, and the gun's report rang in his ears like canon fire as he hit the hay-covered dirt floor, rolling and snatching its barrel, wrenching it from her hands.

She gasped, then wheeled back to protect the man on the floor, throwing her arms across him.

Brandish stood up slowly, and it was only then that the woman blinked and saw past her fears—saw for the first time the white of his skin, the blue of his uniform, and her face changed instantly.

"Thank God you've finally arrived!" she said. "I prayed the army would come." She turned back to the man on the ground. "Help has come, Jonathan . . . thank God, help has come."

But the man did not hear her words.

Brandish watched her gently touch the wounded man's forehead again, fighting back her own exhaustion. Now that he was here, she seemed at once to give in to her immense fatigue, and she leaned her head back against the stall. Brandish grimaced. How to tell her that instead of the United States Cavalry, God had only sent her one retired captain. He leaned the rifle against the wall, beyond her reach.

"When did this happen?"

She looked at him with weary eyes, appearing sunken by the ring of dark encircling them. How many hours had she gone without sleep, he wondered.

"Yesterday morning. They came in the morning—you do have a doctor with you?"

"No."

"No!" She levered herself from the wall, setting her back rigid, her eyes suddenly intense. "But Jonathan is desperately ill. He needs a doctor!"

Brandish reached for the man's forehead. Feverish heat was apparent before his hand touched the burning skin. He frowned at the arrow that had entered beneath the lowest rib and said, "He needs more than a doctor. He needs a surgeon." There was no way to know if the arrow had punctured the stomach or intestines. If it had, even a surgeon would be of little help. "We will have to get him out of here and into the house."

Her face blanched. A quick tongue darted over her dried, cracked lips, and a wild look came instantly to her eyes, warning Brandish that she was fighting a close battle with hysteria. "They're dead. They're all dead, you know," she said, fighting back panic. "Mr. Cohen. His wife, Ruby. The driver. Poor Mr. Waterworth. They're all dead."

He put a hand out to try to calm her. She shrank from it, staring at his fingers as if they had poisonous stingers on their tips. There was something more here than the Apache attack, he suddenly realized. Something terrible had stained this woman's soul. She watched him withdraw the hand as she might a saber's blade being wrenched from her heart, and then she let go of a held breath.

Brandish said, "Yes, I know. I have already been to the house."

She swallowed hard, regaining some composure. "Yes, of course, you would have. Your men must have searched the house for survivors by now." Her tongue licked across her lips again, an odd confusion and a wandering eye seemingly stealing away her sanity a moment. "Yes, you would have . . ." she said again.

He looked down at the wounded man struggling for each ragged breath. Sweat flowed in grimy rivulets over florid cheeks; the dirt beneath his head had been muddied by them—them and the damp compresses she had been applying. The arrow rose and fell, and even though he was unconscious, each breath brought a twitch of pain to the man's pale lips.

Even if the arrow had not punctured stomach or intestine, men did not often survive this kind of wound. In his line of work, Brandish had buried more than his share of strong soldiers who had fallen beneath lesser wounds. This fellow had cheated death longer than most.

The woman's eyes became suddenly clear, her thoughts brought back under control, and she said desperately, "What should we do, then?" Her eyes flashed back and forth between him and the man, as if uncertain where to look. "I have done all I know how."

"You have kept him alive this long. That's saying quite a bit, ma'am. I suspect any internal bleeding has stopped by now."

"Is that hopeful?"

He made a wry grin. "It is . . . in its own small way. But the danger now is not so much the arrow, although it will have to be removed. What threatens him now is the infection, and dehydration—have you been able to get him to drink?"

She nodded her head. "At first he drank almost a full canteen. That was yesterday morning. Then in the afternoon he passed out and I haven't been able to get him to drink any water since."

Brandish held a long breath, considering. It didn't sound good. He released the breath, letting it drain slowly away, and said, "The first thing we have to do is get him out of here. I'll go clean out the station and find something that we can use for a stretcher."

Her eyes flashed, confused. "*You'll* clean the stage station? You are—" She looked at the bars on his shoulders. "—a captain?" She glanced about, seeing for the first time that he was alone, and all at once she seemed to understand. Abruptly she stood and went to the window, and when she turned back the fear had returned to her face. Cautiously, as if she did not really want to hear the answer, she said, "How many men do you have with you, Captain?"

"I am alone. There is no one else with me, ma'am."

"Alone." The word was not much louder than a single breath. She moved away from the window and folded her arms tightly about her waist, struggling suddenly with something within herself. In a moment, the faint quiver in her arms ceased. She swallowed, drawing on some hidden reserve of strength, and looked up sharply. "Very well, Captain. Then it is up to the two of us to care for Jonathan." She swept past him and knelt beside the wounded man again, putting a palm to his burning brow. "Are you familiar with this type of wound?"

"I am. It's not the sort a man generally recovers from," he said bluntly.

His words took her back a moment. She eyed him narrowly and said, "But *he* will survive, Captain."

"Perhaps. I'll see to the stage station now."

When he had gone but a few steps he paused and looked back at her. She had slumped against the wall, gripping herself as if to restrain the convulsions that had returned to wrack her body. The ex–cavalry captain frowned. He had seen this in men before, in men too terrified to shoulder a rifle or draw a saber . . . the look of resignation in the face of a soldier who knew death was only moments away. The look of surrender. A man's—or a woman's—worst enemy.

The encroaching night had overtaken the stage stop when Brandish strode out of the barn and across the yard toward the dark building. His senses were keenly tuned to the sounds of this twilight, but all he heard was the scuff of his own boots and the trickle of the black water to the north of the house. A stair tread creaked beneath his boot as he mounted the porch. He paused to look out over a swiftly fading landscape. The Apaches were still out there, he was certain of that. Somewhere, they were nearby and watching even now.

Then his thoughts returned to what he needed to do next, and with a sudden heaviness of heart, Brandish went inside.

Chapter Four

One by one, Brandish dragged and carried the bodies of Frank and Ruby Cohen out of the house and around to the back of the blacksmith's hut. The two men from the porch were next, then the black man and the dog from the yard, and finally the big blacksmith, Ralph Tabadore. He laid them in a row behind the hut and stared at their dark shapes in the darker shadows for a long, silent moment. They deserved to be buried properly. Later, he promised himself. For now he had to tend to the living—and the one struggling to remain that way.

As he stood there, no longer able to see their faces, his memories of Frank and Ruby were bright and clear, like a magic lantern show he had seen once in St. Louis. He heard Frank Cohen's hearty laughter ringing in his brain, saw his wide, spirited smile, which at times threatened to swallow up his face. And Ruby . . . dear Ruby. The old woman had been like a mother to him out here in the wilds of Arizona. The feel of her rough hand upon his shoulder and the shrill of her voice near his ear, warning him not to believe a word of some tale or another that Frank had told him, was suddenly as substantial and real as if the old woman was even now standing at his elbow.

Frank and Ruby had run the mail stop since before the Butterfield Overland Mail Company had abandoned this southern stretch of their run in 1861 with the coming of the war. Butterfield left the Cohens to fend for themselves, and an admirable job they had done of it, scratching a living out of a wild frontier. During the last three years, while Brandish had been stationed at Camp Lowell, he had made a point of stopping by whenever he could, to check up on them, and to have Frank and Ruby beat him and the blacksmith, or anyone else who happened to be handy, in a game or two of whist.

This was to have been Brandish's final farewell to them—only he hadn't expected to be saying it like this.

He shrugged off his sudden melancholy and rounded up his horse. There was work to do. Brandish started for the empty corrals, but all at once changed his mind, and brought the animal back out front to the overturned stagecoach. He slipped on a halter and tied the leads to the big wheel that now lifted awkwardly toward the night sky. Here, at least, the mare could give out a warning if anyone tried to approach under cover of the darkness.

Back inside the station, Brandish unbarred the second bedroom window, and as a freshening breeze flushed through the room, he went about straightening the bedding, finding lamps, filling them from a can of kerosene, and setting them about to dispel some of the gloom of the place. He gathered up the clutter, swept out the shattered glass and empty shell casings, sprinkled fresh dirt over the blood that had stained the hard-mud floors, and set the furniture around in proper fashion.

Taking up a folded bedsheet and a lamp, Ethan Brandish halted at the door and looked back to survey his handiwork. It would never have passed inspection back at Fort Riley, he mused wryly, but the place was a damn sight better than when he had found it.

The woman wheeled about, a flash of panic in her eyes. Brandish halted just outside the stall and held the light overhead, watching her. The Winchester, he noted, was once again at the woman's side and cocked.

"Oh!" she said, recovering a bit of her tattered composure, "you must forgive me, Captain. I'm afraid my nerves are not what they once were."

"Understandable. You've had yourself a frightful time here, ma'am." He glanced out the dark window at the soft glow now coming from the windows of the house beyond it, then back. "And

I'm afraid it isn't going to get much better... yet."

"You are not a very encouraging man, Captain . . . ?" She paused, pointedly drawing out his rank into a question.

"Brandish," he said. "Ethan Brandish." The lamplight fell full upon her face, and now he was able to see the color of her eyes. Blue. A color that went well with the golden tangles that drooped to her shoulders—tangles at the moment sorely in need of a washing and the attentions of a comb—hair about the color of the dog he had carried out behind the smithy's hut. She was not a pretty woman, but not unpleasant to look at either. She had a plain face with a slightly oversize nose, and her mouth tended to lower on one side of her face when she frowned, which she seemed to be doing a lot of.

There was a frailty about her—not of flesh or bone, more of spirit, he decided. He saw it in the manner her wide eyes watched him, in the tenseness about her whenever he drew too near. All so incongruent with her proud bearing, and the pluck he had detected earlier when she finally understood that help had not arrived in force, but only in the shape of a single man.

Her skin had seen the rigors of wind and sun, and she seemed to know how to handle a rifle. Under different circumstances, she might be a dependable person to have at his side.

"Captain Brandish," she started, and the next moment seemed confused, not sure how to continue. "I . . . I am thankful for your arrival. Please

Brandish

don't misunderstand. When I first saw you—your uniform—I just assumed you were in command of a troop on patrol . . ." She paused and glanced at the wounded man. "I had hoped and prayed so hard . . . I guess I was expecting more."

She looked up abruptly. "My name is Jane. Jane Weston. And this is my—" The hesitation was no more than a catch in her voice, but Brandish heard it. "—My husband, Jonathan."

Brandish let it pass and said, "The stage station isn't exactly up to infirmary standards, but it's better than some field hospitals I've seen. It's airing out now, and the lamps should dispel some of the unpleasantness. I've prepared the bed for your husband."

"That will be fine, Captain Brandish." Her eyes shifted from him to the man on the ground, and narrowed. "How shall we ever move him?"

Brandish handed her the sheet he'd taken from Ruby and Frank's bedroom. "The way we would carry a wounded man off a battlefield. I noticed some coach reins on the wall outside these stalls. You can separate them while I find some poles."

Jane Weston rose with the folded sheet clutched tightly to herself and took the lamp he offered her. There was that cautiousness again in the manner that she approached him, and a swiftness in her steps as she retreated. The lamp's light faded down the aisle between the stalls. Ethan Brandish went out into the chalky moonlight.

Clean, cool desert air outside filled his lungs. He glanced at the house, and the warm glow from its shattered windows. A slight breeze ruffled the tattered remains of Ruby's curtains in the bedroom. In the darkness, the broken glass was not visible, and neither were the bodies behind the smithy's hut. All evidence of yesterday's massacre were neatly hidden by the night—all except the overturned coach out front, where his horse stood watching him.

The darkness hides many things, Brandish reminded himself, redoubling his guard as he moved through the corral and slid out two smooth poles from a gate.

Jane Weston had a pair of reins separated out of the tangled bunch and was working on another when Brandish came back into the barn carrying the poles.

"Spread that sheet out," he said.

She snapped it open in the tight confines of the stall and Brandish laid the poles upon it, two feet apart. He folded the sheet twice around them, then used his sheath knife to punch holes in it. She helped him weave the reins though the sheet and around one of the poles. When he was satisfied it would hold the weight of a man, he and Jane carefully lifted Jonathan onto it.

"You take that end. It'll be lighter," Brandish said, grasping the thick poles at Jonathan's head. "When I give the word, we lift together, and try to keep your husband as level as possible."

Jane Weston gripped the poles. "I'm ready, Captain," she said.

"Now." They stood together. The sheet grew taut and held. "Have you got a firm grip?"

Brandish

"Yes. I'm fine."

"Watch your step, Mrs. Weston." He started out of the stall. Once out in the aisle he slowed so the woman would have no trouble keeping up, and then they were through the side door and outside, angling toward the stage station.

Brandish halted when they reached the station's porch steps. "How are you managing, Mrs. Weston?"

"I'm all right, Captain," she replied, but there was shortness in her breathing, and effort in her words.

"Just a little farther, ma'am." He started up the steps, lowering his end a bit to keep the stretcher level as they mounted the porch. He pushed the door open with the toe of his boot and they scuffled through the house and eased the litter onto the bed.

Working together, they slid the stretcher from beneath Jonathan Weston and Jane carried it out of the bedroom. When she returned, Brandish had his knife out and was already beginning to cut away the shirt that clung to the crusted wound. She took the lamp off the bureau and held it close for him.

"What do you think?" Her voice was soft and cautious above him.

It didn't look good, but then he had already told her that. He said, "We're going to need hot water."

"I'll make a fire," she said, and returned the lamp to the bureau.

* * *

When he stepped from the bedroom a few minutes later, Jane Weston was bent over the firebox, placing sticks expertly about a small flame consuming a wadded-up ball of newsprint.

Seeing him suddenly standing there, she took an involuntary step backward, but recovered almost instantly. "How is he, Captain?"

"Your husband is not in a good way, Mrs. Weston. I'm going to have to cut the arrow out, and that might kill him. It's a safe bet that if I don't try, he'll die anyway."

Jane fought back the wave of despair that showed on her face, and with resolute courage settling in its place, she took up a bucket and said, "I'll go out for water."

"No, you stay here."

Her eyes were instantly wary and shifted toward the closed door. "You think they might still be out there, nearby then?"

"There's no way of knowing. The Apaches are peculiar warriors, and they don't usually leave a job undone without good reason, especially when they have the upper hand. Until I have a chance to do some scouting around, you'll be better off staying inside. Bar the door after me when I leave, and while I'm gone see if you can find soap. Then start cutting bandages from that sheet we carried him over on, and boil them in the water. I'll check the blacksmith's shop for knives and a whetstone."

"Mrs. Cohen had some knives." Jane pulled open a cupboard drawer. "Can you use these?"

Brandish examined the kitchen utensils,

frowning. "I doubt the post surgeon would approve, but they'll do once I put a better edge on them."

At the door, Brandish turned back. "I won't be but a few minutes."

As Brandish left her there, he could not help but feel that in spite of her trepidation, his departure was a welcomed relief from having him so near. She was a confusing woman, he decided, as he loosened his revolver in its holster and stepped out into the night.

Chapter Five

Brandish raised the lamp over his head. Its flickering, yellow light fell upon the hulking black silhouette of the brick furnace in the middle of the hut, and as he moved, the shifting shadows showed him a jumble of heavy tools hanging from wooden pegs on the wall behind a cluttered bench. The dark shape of an anvil rising from the dirt floor occupied one side of the hut, while a tub of water stood nearby.

He began the task of searching the shop, and put out of his mind the thought of the bodies laid out in a line behind the hut, just beyond the wall. He knew what he was looking for, and finally found it on a shelf, shoved in among an assortment of tools the purposes of which he could not even begin to guess.

Brandish pocketed the well-used whetstone.

Brandish

There wasn't anything else here that would have been of use to him for what he needed to do tonight, but as he turned away, his light glinted off of something in a dark corner that gave back an amber flash. Brandish moved aside a jagged sheet of iron plate and retrieved a half-full bottle of whiskey. He grinned. It was Ralph's private stash, and he tucked it under his arm as he left the blacksmith's hut.

Outside, he halted where the bodies lay and the grin became a grimace. He would see to their burial in the morning, and when he did, the chances were good there would be one more added to their number.

Brandish looked out across the yard, beyond the corrals. Moonlight touched the smooth surface of the nearby pond, but darkness crouched about its edges, and gathered beneath the overhang of cottonwood trees where the chalky light could not reach. Crickets and toads sang undisturbed. The ex–cavalry captain made note of their sound, impressing it upon his brain before he went down to the water to fill the bucket. As he started away, he was mindful of the sudden stillness by the pond, and he impressed that upon his brain as well.

Back at the stage station he mounted the porch, then remembered the horse he had left tied out front.

The animal's tail swept lazily, its ears hitched forward at him. Brandish loosened the halter leads from the stage wheel and brought the horse to the station, tying it off on the porch railing.

He went around back to the barn for a fork of hay, then unsaddled the animal, heaved the light McClellan over the railing, and took his blanket, saddlebags, and saber into the house with him.

Jane Weston was feeding more wood into the stove when Brandish came through the door. He could see the effort she exerted to fortify herself now that he had returned. "Did you find what you were looking for?" she asked him, standing.

He put the bucket of water by the stove and removed the whetstone from the pocket of his blouse. "Yes," he said setting the stone on the table with the bottle of whiskey he had discovered.

Her eyes suddenly narrowed and a quaver came to her voice. "Is that yours?"

He grinned, and thought he was beginning to understand now what it might be that was troubling the lady. "No, ma'am. It belonged to Mr. Tabadore, the blacksmith. His private supply, I suspect. You see, Ruby Cohen didn't hold with spiritous drinks in her house. Mr. Tabadore had it hidden away in a corner out in the shop." The grin faded. "But by the time we finish up with what we need to do here tonight, I'll wager both you and I will be needing a sip or two of it—that is, if there's any left over."

"What do you mean, left over?"

"Sterilization, ma'am. For cleaning the wound. That's all I mean."

"Oh," she said, but her tenseness remained.

He said, "I know for a fact that Ruby Cohen had a sewing basket around here someplace. Perhaps you can find it for me while I get to work on these knives."

Jane Weston nodded and turned away, then suddenly back. "You seem to know what you're doing, Captain Brandish." She attempted to make it sound like a simple observation, but he knew there was more to it than that. She was looking for some encouragement, for what needed to be done next. "I mean, a man with your background would have had experience with this sort of thing . . . ?"

He had—a lifetime's worth—and he grimaced as he set to work on the kitchen knives. "Ever hear of the Battle of Beecher's Island, ma'am?" he asked, sliding the blade across the stone.

"No . . . I don't think so."

"Well, I'm not surprised. It wasn't a very noteworthy battle I suppose, not unless you happened to be in the middle of it. Every battle is noteworthy when it's your hide being shot at. I was at Fort Hays. Temporary duty. We were a party of fifty under Major George Forsyth. 'First-class hardy frontiersmen' he had called us when we rode away from the fort that day. The trail we were following was Sioux—or so we thought. It turned out there was a number of Cheyenne and Arapaho among them as well. We had just crossed the Arikaree River when they attacked—more than six hundred of them—all experienced Plains warriors.

"To our good fortune, Forsyth had suspected the trap they'd laid for us. He regrouped us on an island in the Arikaree. We dug in behind our horses and opened up on them with repeating Spencer rifles. In that first charge, we managed to split them as they reached the river, dividing them around the island. Our surgeon, John Mooers, was hit. So was Forsyth. In the second charge their leader, a huge Cheyenne named Roman Nose, was killed and they pulled back to regroup, giving us time to fortify our position and assess our loses. Twenty-one men were hit, sixteen of them with survivable wounds. Our surgeon died in that first volley and that left just us fighting men to tend to the wounded."

Brandish paused and looked up at her. "That afternoon I cut out six arrows and I can't remember how many bullets." His voice suddenly turned grave. "To be truthful, Mrs. Weston, not one of those wounds was as serious as your husband's, and those that were had already done their intended work."

She flinched. "It must have been awful."

"No more so than what you went through yesterday morning. For the man, or the woman, behind the rifle, every battle is the worst battle. It's only the smug historians, comfortable and safe in their libraries years later, that tell us this battle or that one was the worst, or this one more significant than the one that came just before, or followed right after."

For several seconds neither spoke. Brandish resumed lapping the knife across the sharpening stone. She watched him a moment longer and then turned away to search for Ruby Cohen's sewing basket.

Brandish

* * *

The whistling teapot broke the silence that had settled within the close walls of the stage station, summoning Jane from the bedroom to tend to it. She placed a small wicker basket on the table at Brandish's elbow in passing, and removed the steaming pot from the stove.

Brandish set aside the knives and rummaged through the basket, removing spools of thread. He found a wrist cushion, prickly like a porcupine with all of Ruby's sewing needles stuck into it. He gathered up what he thought he'd need and put it all into an iron pot, bringing them to the stove. "Get these boiling, Mrs. Weston, and keep them there for fifteen minutes. Have you begun to wash around the wound yet?"

"No, not yet," she said, filling another pot with water from the pail and setting it atop the stove. "But I'll do it now." She turned back to the bedroom.

He reached out and stopped her. "I'll see to it."

She eyed his large hand about her arm, and stiffened ever so slightly. Brandish released her gently and she stepped back, opening the distance between them.

"You're tighter than a fiddle string, ma'am. Why don't you sit and rest for a little while? I'm going to need you alert when I start to work on your husband."

Jane Weston drew herself up tall and straight, her eyes suddenly hardened, like chips of blue flint. "I'm all right, I assure you, Captain. I'll help you with Jonathan now." She grabbed up the towels that she had set aside for the task.

"As you wish."

He carried the hot water, soap, and a small empty bowl into the bedroom and set a lamp on a nightstand nearby. The soap and water loosened the dried blood crusted into the material of the shirt that Brandish had not been able to remove earlier. He peeled the softened cloth away and cleaned the feverish skin around the shaft of the Apache arrow.

The infection was deep and spreading.

Jane looked away and composed herself.

"You've not seen anything quite like this?" he asked matter-of-factly, not looking up.

"No. It's nothing like the accidents that sometimes occur around a ranch, Captain. The slip of a knife or the glancing blow of an ax can make a horrible wound, but they are tended to at once, not allowed to fester. No, I've not seen anything quite like this."

"Well, you best look at it and get used to it. His survival may well hinge on the steadiness of your hand, Mrs. Weston."

"My hand?"

"This is going to take the both of us."

She looked back at the wound.

"The queasiness will pass in a minute or two. Think of it as one of those ranch accidents you mentioned, and not what it really is."

"That's easier said than done, Captain."

"Yes, ma'am."

There was a flash in her eyes, then she said, "Tell me what you want me to do."

Brandish

Brandish dabbed away the last of the dried blood from the painted wooden shaft and studied the puncture with a practiced eye. His tour of duty in the West had steeled him to such injuries, and at the same time had made him somewhat of an authority on battle wounds. The skin was an angry red, webbed with ugly, radiating fingers of pus. It had already begun to close back around the arrow. Deadly infection was spreading. For Jane Weston's sake, he refrained from frowning, and removed his watch from his pocket. The cover snapped open—9:50. He handed it up to her.

"Make certain the needles and knives boil a full fifteen minutes. You can keep time with my watch. In the meanwhile, bring me that whiskey."

She returned a moment later clutching the bottle in both hands.

Brandish poured some around the wound, then half filled the small bowl.

He noted the time again when she had carried the steaming pot into the bedroom and handed his watch back to him—10:05. With a pair of canning tongs, Brandish transferred the knives, needles, and thread to the bowl of whiskey.

Jane moved a second lamp nearer. "Are we ready?" she asked softly.

Brandish nodded his head and fished up a sharpened knife from the bowl. Shaking the whiskey from it, he looked up and saw in her eyes that she understood the long shot they were gambling on. Just the same, there was no other option left to them. He was aware, also, of a certain sternness developing about Jane Weston; the same determination he'd briefly noticed in her before.

She moved closer, holding the lamp near, and Brandish heard her breath catch as the knife in his fingers touched the festering skin.

Chapter Six

Brandish stared at the white enameled face of his watch, but his thoughts were elsewhere, not comprehending the position of the gold hands.

Exhaustion.

The sudden drain at a battle's end.

The long, tension-filled wait for the next attack.

He had experienced them all before—in different places, under different circumstances—but the feelings were always the same. The pale lamplight played across his tired face. His fingers still tingled from the feel of the cold steel between them, and the warm flow of blood over them.

"What time is it?" Jane Weston asked, her voice an unwanted intrusion into his thoughts. Her exhaustion seemed equal to his own.

"Ma'am?" he asked, and blinked up at her, coming out of his hypnotic gaze.

"The time. You've been staring at that watch for most of five minutes now, Captain."

"Oh." Brandish shook his head, clearing the cobwebs, and glanced back at the gold watch open in his palm. "Good Lord, it's already one-thirty?"

Jane sat wearily in the chair across the table from him. "Has it really been three and a half hours?" Her breath escaped in a long sigh. "It feels an eternity."

Brandish snapped the lid down and shoved the watch back into his pocket. "Have you checked in on him?"

"I just changed the cloth on his forehead. He's burning up."

"It's the infection. His body is trying to kill it with heat. The trouble being, that same heat works both ways. It may kill him in the process." He stood up from the chair, stretched, and stepped to the bedroom.

Jane Weston came up behind him. "I'm going to sit up with him, Captain. Why don't you get some sleep?"

Brandish shook his head and turned away from the doorway, staring now at the shuttered window. "No, I'll stay up a while longer," he said, hearing the exhaustion in his voice. He lifted the cross bolt and opened the shutter. A cool breeze relieved some of the stuffiness in the closed-up stage station, but it invigorated him very little.

Brandish

In the waning light of a low half moon, the trees down by the pond cast shadows that reached nearly to the station. Brandish listened to the small sounds of crickets and toads coming from that direction for a while. Out front, his horse lifted its head, watched him a moment, and lowered it again sleepily.

How long, he wondered. *Perhaps tomorrow morning—perhaps the next . . . perhaps never. . . .*

He heard her come up behind him again. When he turned, Jane Weston took a startled step backward. At arm's length she handed him the steaming cup of coffee.

"You look like you can use this."

The tension had returned to her voice. He sensed her struggle—but what was it that Jane Weston was battling? Her own exhaustion? Her fear? Perhaps both—and perhaps something else entirely. He had a hunch that whatever it was, it went further back than the attack on the stage station two days ago—well, three days now, he corrected himself.

She said, "If I'm to spend the night at Jonathan's side, I'm going to need this." She sat back at the table, setting her own cup before her. He closed the shutters and joined her.

"Tastes good," he said, staring over the smoky lamp on the table. Its yellow light revealed a haggard woman who had somehow lost her youth long before it was time. She required a bath, as did he. Her oily hair needed washing and combing, and the torn and dirty white dress looked gray now, and needed to be replaced with something clean and gay. But there was something else here that clean clothes and soapy water could never bring back. Whatever had happened to Jane Weston had left an indelible black stain on her soul.

Jane Weston would never be beautiful, yet Brandish had no doubt that beneath the grime and ruined clothes there lurked an attractive and confident woman—but she was not going to show him that side of herself . . . at least not yet.

"You had a hard time with it, Captain. Removing the arrow didn't go well, did it?" she asked.

He frowned and glanced down into his coffee cup. "Frankly, I don't know what has kept him alive this long. It's one of those mysteries, ma'am. One man will scratch himself on a wire fence and be dead in three days, another will get himself shot full of bullets and arrows and survive. There's no accounting for it."

"He will live," she said with a surety of conviction that made Brandish wonder briefly what soothsayer she had been in touch with.

Brandish hid his grimace behind a sip of coffee. "I certainly hope so, ma'am. I'm not a prophet or a doctor. I can't predict things like that. So far, your husband has managed to survive a wound that would have killed other men. Maybe he's stronger than most, maybe he's just lucky, or maybe . . . well, there's no way to know these things. We'll just have to wait and see."

"Then I shall keep on praying."

"At the moment, that's all we can do. That, and maybe getting him to drink some water."

Brandish

Jane stood immediately and went into the bedroom. Brandish rose after a minute and watched her from the doorway, trying to get water between Jonathan's lips.

"Here, let me show you," he said, rolling a scrap of the bedsheet they had cut into bandages into a thin cigar. "Put this between his teeth."

She did as he asked. Brandish poured a little water onto it. "Now all you have to do is keep it damp. His mouth will absorb the moisture."

"One of those battlefield lessons?"

He grinned. "Actually, it's an old Apache way of dealing with the problem. I learned it from one of our scouts."

She frowned. "I don't think I ever did approve of Indians working for the cavalry."

"The best way to know how an enemy thinks is to hire some of them. Besides, it takes an Apache to catch an Apache, and it's demoralizing to have their own people fighting for the other side. Crook pretty much pioneered the idea."

"They would do that? Fight against their own people? What about loyalty to their nation?"

"Nation?" Brandished laughed. "Very loosely speaking, I suppose you can call them a nation. They're more like extended families. The Apaches are spread over a vast territory with only rudimentary connections with each other. There's little to hold them together. Little of what you might call a tribal mentality. For the most part, they're isolated family groups, each led by the strongest or wisest man among them. There's some communication between the southern, central, and eastern groups, but it's fragmented at best, and it isn't hard to find Apaches willing to work for the government. And when they do, they're loyal soldiers, and ruthless against their own people.

"Anyway, it's only a few Indians making a fuss. That's the way it's been with most of these campaigns. Only a few make the trouble, and the rest suffer for it."

"I didn't know."

He smiled wearily. "Well, you're not alone. It seems that most of the lead-headed congressmen we've elected to run this country don't know that either."

"Well, I suppose you learn about such things working in this country," she answered, vaguely defensive.

"All too well, ma'am," he said with a grin. Then he became serious again. "Can you tell me what happened here, Mrs. Weston?"

She stepped past him into the main room and held the coffee cup between her palms, as if to warm her hands, staring at something only she could see. "You mean the attack?" she asked at length, her words strangely remote.

"Do you have any idea what provoked the Apaches?"

She turned on him abruptly, her eyes wide. "Do Indians *need* a reason?"

Brandish was surprised at the sudden venom in her voice. He said evenly, "They most often do, though their reasons may not make a whole lot of sense to you or me. But then, much of what we do doesn't make much sense to the Apaches either."

Her anger flared. "You can stand there and defend those murdering red savages, Captain Brandish? After what they did here?"

"I don't defend murderers—no matter what the color of their skin."

Jane Weston's eyes bore down on him, and in her disheveled state, Brandish had the odd notion that if she were only to change the color of her eyes and hair, and her clothing, she wouldn't be all that different from the Apache women he'd seen in the lodges along the Tonto Basin.

He said, "It wasn't but seven years ago, and I was fighting a different sort of enemy, in places with names like Gettysburg, or Vicksburg. The fighting then wasn't all that much different than now, ma'am, and now as then, it only makes good military sense to understand your enemy. That's what I try to do with the Apaches."

"I hate Indians!" Her words were brittle and cold, like the icicles that for most of the long winter used to hang from the eaves of the post headquarters of his first Western assignment, in the Dakota Territory.

"It was only a few Apaches that did this," he pointed out reasonably. "Cochise and his people are on the Chiricahua Reservation, and most of the Coyoteros, the Apaches that attacked this station, are on the reservation at Camp Verde."

"I don't care. I hate them all!"

He started to object, but then he realized that in her frayed state it would do little good to list

Douglas Hirt

all the tribes that wanted peace and a closer relationship with the torrent of white men flooding into the West over the Oregon, the Santa Fe, and the Bozeman trails, and along the Smoky Hill Road, and a dozen others like it. He could not convince her that there were any good Indians in this wild country—and he wasn't going to try.

A moment of silence passed, and then Jane Weston let her anger die. Not looking at him, but again staring at that thing only she could see, she said, "They came from the west—I think. It's all rather hazy now. It was morning. About seven I think. No way to be sure."

"That would be about right. The Apaches usually attack early. Why don't you sit down, Mrs. Weston?"

She looked at him with a start, and after a moment nodded her head and lowered herself into a chair at the table. Brandish brought the coffeepot over and filled both their cups.

"Mrs. Cohen was cleaning up the breakfast dishes, and the Negro, Ben, he and my—" Her voice stumbled. "—my husband went out to the barn to look at the mules that he had brought by the evening before for the relays. He had a horse camp somewhere nearby here, he told us. He raised horses and mules to sell to the stage company, and whoever else, I suppose."

"Ben Smith?" Brandish asked.

"Yes, that was him. You knew him?"

Brandish shook his head. "Never personally met the man, but his name has appeared on requisitions. The cavalry had bought horses from him from time to time."

Jane went on. "We used to raise horses—my husband and I. We had us a little place along the Canadian River in eastern New Mexico Territory, near the Texas border. So it was just natural that Jonathan was interested in Ben's stock, and Ben Smith was a friendly man, eager to show them off. He had an absolutely delightful laugh that sounded like it began in the bottom of a barrel. . . .

"Well, anyway, like I was saying, Jonathan and Ben had just gone out back to the barns, and the stage driver, Hank Cloy, and Frank Cohen—they were busy out front harnessing fresh animals to the stage for the morning run."

She looked at Brandish, her eyes gathering tears that made them glisten in the lamplight. "I was inside with Mrs. Cohen, feeding table scraps to that beautiful dog of Mr. Smith's when they attacked us. It came so suddenly, there really isn't much to tell, Captain. I tried to help, but there were no guns about. Frank Cohen had his with him. Frank made it back to the station somehow.

"Hank Cloy had a revolver. I could hear it booming out on the porch. Mr. Waterworth, the other passenger, he was unarmed. There was a shotgun in the coach, but we couldn't get to it after the attack began. Mr. Waterworth tried. He was the first to die.

"I remember . . . looking out the back window

... seeing my—seeing Jonathan come out of the barn with a revolver..."

That faraway look had returned to her eyes.

"It was at that moment that he was shot. The next thing I knew, Mr. Smith had come from the barn and was carrying him back inside." Jane fell silent and brushed at her eyes.

With a faint smile she said, "The next instant Mr. Smith dove out of the doorway with his rifle and rolled under the corral poles. It was curious the way he moved. Almost as if he knew exactly which direction the attack would come from next. As if... as if he had fought Indians before. For a while they could not get near him. He had managed to clear a corridor to the stage station, and was making his way toward it, to help us trapped here inside.... That's when he ran out of bullets. It was only then that the savages were able to get close enough to... to..." Her voice dropped off.

"Of course, by that time it was only Mrs. Cohen and me left. The others were all dead. Hank had tried to help Mr. Waterworth. He didn't make it. Then a bullet came through the back window and Mrs. Cohen died. I can't remember much after that."

Jane Weston crawled back inside her thoughts. Ethan Brandish spent a long moment pondering the story she had just told him, and listening to the wind moving around outside, wondering briefly if it really was the wind. But his horse remained quiet.

There was still something missing—some-

Brandish

thing that she had not yet mentioned, something that might solve the puzzle that had troubled him since his arrival. . . .

"Tell me, Mrs. Weston, why did the Apaches leave so suddenly?"

Chapter Seven

Jane Weston looked up at him, surprised. "How could you know that?"

"They didn't take scalps. They didn't mutilate any bodies. You and your husband are still alive. That would not have happened, Mrs. Weston, unless something had occurred to make the Apaches leave here in a hurry."

"I hadn't really thought about it," she said, "but you're correct, Captain. They did leave suddenly. I just assumed it was because they had done what they had come to do and left. Afterward, I was too busy tending to Jonathan to wonder about it."

"Can you remember anything unusual that happened, Mrs. Weston?"

She laughed suddenly, bitterly. "*Unusual?* You mean something more unusual that being attacked by Apaches and seeing everyone around you murdered? No, Captain Brandish, I really can't think of anything more unusual than that."

Brandish grimaced and nodded his head. "Your point's well taken. Let me rephrase—"

"No. No need. I quite understood what you meant. I'm sorry, I guess I'm tired. I didn't mean to be short with you, Captain." She shook her head and stared wearily at the coffee remaining in the bottom of her cup. "No. I can't think of anything that would have caused the Indians to leave like they did. I do remember that after Ben had been killed, and only I was left, how desperate I felt knowing that surely I was going to die any moment too. I'd heard the stories, you understand. I've read the accounts of Indian massacres, even seen an ambrotype of one, so I sort of knew what to expect next."

She stopped and licked her lips slowly, as if to allow her tongue to explore individually each of the dried cracks that had opened there these last few desperate days.

"I think," she went on, thoughtfully, "that I must have felt it would be better to die quickly, fighting them, than to go through that horror again—"

She stopped suddenly and averted her eyes. "I mean . . . I don't know what I mean. I don't know what prompted me to do it. Perhaps it was the valiant way that Mr. Smith had died. I don't know. I remember throwing open the back door and running out to where Ben had fallen. His dog was standing over the body, barking, not allowing anyone near the fallen man, but for some reason he allowed me to come near. I pulled the rifle from under Ben's body. The next thing I remember, the dog was crying horribly. When I looked, the poor animal had been pinned to the ground by a spear, its legs thrashing as it tried desperately to free itself.

"I remember hearing shots all around me, and there were arrows too, and I knew I was about to die . . . but at that moment I don't think I even cared." She looked at Brandish earnestly, and concern was suddenly in her eyes. "Does that make any sense to you, Captain? Knowing you're about to die, but not caring?"

He'd been watching her closely, trying to determine what she was really telling him. Was there something between the words that perhaps she did not realize herself? He said, "It's quite common in the heat of battle to disregard one's own safety and to view death in a detached, almost philosophical way. I shouldn't worry too much about it."

Jane Weston seemed to find some comfort in that. "Well, at least I'm not going crazy."

"No. It's all quite normal when you consider the circumstances." But the question of her sanity was something he wondered about himself. "Go on with what happened next."

She thought back again. "Well, I can remember quite clearly that poor dog. It was whimpering pitifully, and kicking, not being able to free itself. I shiver to think of it. And I remember myself very methodically working the lever on Mr.

Smith's rifle. I didn't know how many bullets he had managed to put into it before he had died, but I knew there was at least one. I could see it through the open bolt before I closed the lever. I was certain I'd have only one chance before I'd be dead, too, so I picked out a target and put everything out of mind except what I'd been taught about shooting a rifle. It all seemed to happen so slow, and precise, like putting a stitch in a garment. The man I was aiming at was quite gaudily dressed. He wore a dirty, blue bandanna about his head. It was decorated with feathers and sticks—or at least something that looked like sticks."

"Bones?"

"Maybe. He had on a vest of some sort, fashioned out of what appeared to be porcupine quills. Beneath it was a long, dirty, yellow shirt. I remember aiming right at the middle of that vest, and then squeezing the trigger, and feeling the rifle thump against my shoulder. . . ." She became silent and Brandish knew she was reliving that very moment. When she continued, her voice had become a whisper. "I recall now how odd everything seemed. Immediately after I fired, I got the impression of everything around me suddenly coming to a halt. I didn't wait to find out why, but I shot again, and another Indian fell. Then I ran back to the station. But the shooting and the war cries had come to a stop, and the Indians began to leave, taking their dead with them. . . ."

She gave him a thin, watered-down smile. "It's

funny, but I never stopped to think about that until right now, until you asked."

Brandish stood and turned toward the shuttered window, staring as if it were open wide and he could all at once see clearly what lay beyond it.

"What's wrong?" Jane asked.

It was suddenly all so clear. Ethan Brandish knew that he must waste no time getting Jane Weston, and the wounded man in the next room, away from there. Fort Bowie was the closest military outpost. They'd have to leave at once.

But they could not leave at once, not without killing the man lying in Frank and Ruby's bed. And besides, how was he going to carry them safely out of there? He frowned. With only one horse, they could not hope to make Fort Bowie before the Apaches returned, and Ethan Brandish, U.S. Cavalry, retired, knew now that the Apaches would return. Perhaps as soon as the morning. They had already been away longer than he would have thought.

"What is it?" she asked again, more urgently.

"I had a feeling that was it," he said at length, falling again into an introspective silence.

"What are you talking about, Captain?"

Brandish made a wry smile and turned away from the window. Jane Weston had come suddenly alert, watching him with wide, distressed eyes, wondering, perhaps, what new peril had befallen her. He said, "You pick good targets, Mrs. Weston."

"What do you mean?"

Brandish

"I mean, the man you killed was a superb choice. His name was Yellow Shirt. You killed their war chief."

Her quick, wary eyes searched his face for an explanation.

"You see, Mrs. Weston, when the war chief is killed in battle, the warriors usually draw back to select another to lead them. Generally, that doesn't take much time. I've seen them back in battle in as little as a quarter hour. Of course, that was when a lesser leader than Yellow Shirt was slain.

"Yellow Shirt, on the other hand, was a mighty important fellow among the Apaches—at least the Coyoteros. He, along with Goyakla, and one or two others, are the last remaining war chiefs and medicine men. I suspect that if Yellow Shirt had been killed by a man, they would have taken considerable less time to find a replacement. That could explain the delay."

"A man? What difference should it make who killed this . . . this Yellow Shirt?"

Brandish went back to the window and opened the shutters. His horse's head came up at the sound of it. The ex–cavalry captain glanced along the porch and out into the blackness that lay beyond. He closed and barred it again and turned back to Jane Weston.

"A man would have been a fitting opponent for a leader of Yellow Shirt's stature. To have died in battle at the hands of a man would have been no disgrace. Being killed by a woman, however . . . well, that's something else again. They see it as bad medicine, and a mighty poor omen. Your killing Yellow Shirt broke the medicine of the battle, and it's going to take a lot of time, and chanting, and praying to get it all back again.

"I don't understand it all myself, but it has to do with Yellow Shirt's spirit and sending it off to the next life. Afterward, when they get the medicine back and they pick a new leader, they're going to have to decide what they're going to do about it." Brandish grinned. "Like I said, you picked good targets."

Her eyes grew intense. "What does that mean for us . . . for me?"

He pulled thoughtfully at his mustache a moment. "I suspect that there might be a few Apaches up in those hills behind the station, keeping an eye on you, Mrs. Weston."

She looked over her shoulder at the shuttered window, then back. "Me? But why me? I was only trying to defend myself! Surely they understand that?"

"That's true, but it doesn't change the fact that *you* killed Yellow Shirt."

Jane Weston seemed to shrink as she leaned back into the chair.

Brandish said, "I can't say with a surety what their medicine man will come up with, but knowing the Apaches' way of thinking, I'd guess that in order to properly truck Yellow Shirt's spirit off to the next world, it's going to require that one of his warriors kills you, Mrs. Weston, and presents your scalp to their gods."

Her face drained of color. "Is that the only

Brandish

way?" Her voice was not much above a whisper.

"Like I said, it's only a guess. It might take an entirely different turn. It might require some act of bravery on the part of one of the warriors, or the new leader. Or Yellow Shirt's death may not be a consideration at all, and for all we know, they all might be fifty miles from here right now."

Jane Weston remained silent, staring, her head shaking slowly from side to side. "But you don't really believe that, do you?"

"No, ma'am. My feeling is they'll be coming back, and it's you they'll be coming back for."

Her wide eyes shifted to the barred and shuttered window and fixed upon it, unblinking.

"But I doubt they'll bother us tonight," Brandish went on. "I left my horse tied out front. If anyone comes around, we'll know about it."

She looked at him with a sudden hopeful glint in her eyes. "You're alone at the moment, but certainly you're expecting to meet up with your troops shortly? They must be on patrol somewhere nearby and will be coming back—?"

She must have seen it on his face. Her words came to a halt and then she said, "There is no patrol? You really are alone?"

"I really am alone."

Despair settled in her voice. "I had hoped there would be others along later."

"As far as I know, there will be no others. When I left Fort Lowell two days ago there was a dispatch from Lieutenant Colonel Crook warning that Yellow Shirt had come out of hiding and was making trouble, but I have no idea how the new captain or the colonel will proceed on it."

"The new captain?"

Brandish smiled slightly. It was bound to come out eventually, and with all the bad news Jane Weston had heard already, this much more would make little difference. He said, "You see, Mrs. Weston, I just retired. I'm no longer in the cavalry . . . officially, that is. Other than my first sergeant back at the fort, no one even knows that I'm here. No, ma'am, I shouldn't expect any help from the army."

Chapter Eight

Ethan Brandish paused in the doorway of the bedroom. Jane Weston seemed at once to sense his presence there and looked over, holding the cup of water from which she'd been carefully dampening the cloth between Jonathan Weston's teeth. In that moment, with Jane and Jonathan close together, Brandish couldn't help but note the remarkable resemblance between the pair. The same color hair, the shape of the jaw ... more than coincidence? Brandish had heard that after a man and woman had lived together long enough, they began to resemble each other. He had always rather doubted the truth of that, but just the same, if there was any, neither Jane nor Jonathan were old enough to have been married that long.

"He's still burning up with fever, Captain," she said.

"Well, all we can do for him now is continue giving him water and try to keep his head cool." Brandish was amazed that Jonathan Weston had managed to hang on this long. He was beginning to wonder if the man might not pull through after all.

Jane returned to her task of dripping water onto the cloth and said, "Can we have any hope at all of help arriving, Captain Brandish?"

"Eventually," he said. "The stage line will certainly send riders to find out what happened to their coach. But that could take some time. No doubt word of Yellow Shirt's recent activity will have already reached the pockets of civilization along the line, and the stage company will surely want to protect their interests, even though these stops are now independently owned. Just the same, it will take time to organize armed parties, or to enlist the help of the cavalry, which I suspect is pretty busy at the moment."

"But we don't have a lot of time," she objected. "In a week we all may be dead."

"That's true, ma'am."

Her head came sharply around. "You don't sound too concerned, Captain."

"There you're mistaken. I am concerned. I have no great desire to die anytime soon. I was sort of looking forward to my retirement, to doing a little of what I wanted to do for a change, not what Colonel Shipton or Lieutenant Colonel Crook tells me I have to do. The fact is, Mrs. Weston, there's not much you or I can do about this situation now, and getting worked up over what may or may not happen tomorrow will get us nowhere. At the moment, we have a man here, teetering on death's doorstep, and I'd say he's our immediate concern."

She looked back at Jonathan's face, splotched red with fever, his sweat soaking the pillow beneath his head. "You're right, captain. I'm not, however, able to hide my fears as well as you."

"I've had more practice," he said, giving her a smile.

For an instant a grin reshaped her face into something pretty and happy, and then it vanished and the worried frown returned.

He strode back to the table, picked up the coffee cup, discovered it empty, and set it down. Unexpectedly, he had discovered a new puzzle here.

Jane came from the other room a moment later and reached for the cup. "Let me refill it for you—"

He put out his hand to stop her and the soft warmth of her flesh beneath it began to tremble. "No, I don't want any more," he said, instantly aware of the cautious way she withdrew her hand, and the distance that immediately opened between them. She stared at him with cold and vaguely terrified eyes. Suddenly he understood what it was that so tormented her . . . and there was something else too that he should have noticed immediately, but hadn't. Jane Weston wore no ring on the finger of her left hand, and judging from the even tan of her skin, there had never been one there.

Brandish said, "There's something I want to check on outside, ma'am." He snatched his saber off a hook, half withdrew it from its scabbard, frowned, and changed his mind, thrusting the weapon back, returning it to the peg on the wall by the door. "I'll be away for a while. Make sure you bar the door after me."

"But where are you going?" she asked, suddenly tense. That was an odd change, he thought. The last time she had been almost eager for him to leave.

"Out to have a look around." He removed the spurs from his cavalry boots and tossed them aside.

"Now?"

"I'll try not to be too long."

Brandish stepped outside, closed the door behind him, and waited until he heard the bar slide heavily into place. He lingered on the porch, gazing out at the shadows by the pond, allowing his eyes to grow accustomed to the dark, listening. His horse lifted its head and watched him. Beyond the animal the overturned stagecoach was a dark lump in the otherwise smooth blackness. Somewhere out of the darkness came the hoot of an owl. Brandish went down the steps, and as he strode around the station, crossing the open ground to the barns, he worked the puzzle over in his brain, but every way he looked at it, the answer always came back the same.

Brandish stopped between the buildings and

looked back at the lines of light filtering through the closed shutters. His frown deepened and he resumed his march to the barns.

There was no getting around it. Jane Weston was a liar.

The waning light from a moon now low on the horizon filtered into the dusty barn through the glassless window where Brandish had first spied Jane Weston earlier that evening. The Winchester rifle still leaned against the wall where she had left it. He worked the lever and ejected four shells. Added to the three he had removed from Ben Smith's dead fingers, that made seven rounds. He fed them all back into the magazine and jacked one up into the chamber, lowering the hammer. He glanced around and found his own Springfield carbine half buried under some hay. In his saddlebags was the standard issue of forty rounds of .45-.55 carbine ammunition and another twenty rounds of .45 for his revolver. Not much in the way of firepower, he mused, brushing the fragments of hay from the Springfield.

He made his way through the darkness, along the line of empty stalls, and found a saddle tossed over one of them with a pair of saddlebags across the seat. There was weight to the bags when he picked them up and carried them to the window, where he untied the flaps in the moonlight. One of the bags contained a hunk of jerked beef wrapped in brown paper, and the other a military cartridge box filled with rifle cartridges, and a large butcher knife. He looked back at the cartridge box, and his lips drew into a tight, thoughtful line for a moment before his thoughts returned to practical matters.

The extra ammunition would make the Winchester more useful, yet Brandish knew he was woefully unprepared for the Apaches when they returned.

But would they return?

He stepped outside the barn and gazed at the black rising land behind them. Well, there was only one way to find out.

Grabbing up the Springfield, Brandish started into the hills, keeping to the deeper shadows, avoiding the skyline. Atop the first ridge he looked back at the dark outline of the stage station below. The corrals strung out behind it, part adobe, part rails, appeared like bleached bones in the moonlight. A splash of chalky light marked the smooth surface of the pond. Nearby was the black rectangle of the blacksmith's hut. Slivers of yellow light escaped the shuttered windows where Jane Weston and her husband were holed up in the station.

Brandish continued up over the ridge and down into a valley beyond that ran mostly north and south. For perhaps a mile he followed it higher into the hills, and suddenly he came to a stop and hunched down into the blackness to wait for the sound of his own footsteps to fade from his ears.

Brandish

The slight breeze coming off the higher land carried with it no warning sounds, but it did bear a message of a different nature.

Wood smoke!

Brandish crept upward, like a stalking animal now, moving soundlessly. He had left the saber behind for just this reason. In some respects it was the most silent of weapons, but dang the thing, it did more often than not get in the way, and it was impossible to keep from rattling with all of its rings and buckles. Despite the flare it lent to a dress uniform, the saber was an archaic holdover from another era, and unless properly instructed in the art of edged warfare, only one soldier in a hundred could use it the way it was meant to be used.

In five minutes, Brandish had located them. Three Apaches, asleep by the embers of a dying campfire. They had not bothered to post guards. No reason to, really. The lone woman down below could never have found them tucked away in this fold of land—even if she had thought to come looking. And apparently they were still unaware of his arrival. That was just as well. It added an advantage. It was always useful to have the enemy underestimate your strength.

Brandish grinned where he lay in the shadows. He had learned the answer to at least one of his questions. The Apaches would be coming back. These three were here only to keep an eye on the stage station until the rest of the band returned with their new leader.

Douglas Hirt

The wind shifted. A horse whinnied. Brandish scudded down into the valley again before the horses could reveal his presence, and made his way back to the stage station.

Chapter Nine

She squeezed the precious moisture from the damp rag, and with each drop that fell into Jonathan's mouth, Jane Weston's hopes sank a little further beneath the weight of mounting despair.

Please, Jonathan, don't die, she chanted softly, gazing upon the horribly red flesh of his burning face. Every few minutes her efforts would be rewarded with the flutter of an eyelid or an involuntary swallow, and then just as swiftly as the new hope had surfaced, it would sink again to new despair.

I don't know what I would do without you—without your strength, Jonathan.

Jane continued at the task for perhaps another hour—she had no way of knowing how long it had been—her fears a mixed bag of concerns. Her thoughts leaped from Jonathan one moment to Ethan Brandish the next. Where had he gone? Had he left her alone, deciding the more prudent action was to ride away now, in the dark, rather than to wait until morning when the Apaches would return?

A sudden shiver raced up her spine and she reached to the bedstead for support. In truth, Jane Weston knew she could not blame Brandish if he did leave. Why should he stay? After all, he was no longer in the cavalry; he had no official obligation to protect them. He had said himself that he was looking forward to retirement. His staying here now would certainly be nothing less than a death wish, and Jane did not think Brandish was a man to be harboring such notions.

She glanced out the bedroom doorway.

How long had he been away?

She wished he had left his watch . . . but of course he would not have done that. He had no intention of returning now.

All at once she had a thought: If his horse was still tied up out front, it would mean he really did intend to return!

Her sudden elation seesawed to low despair. For her to determine if the horse was still out front meant that she had to unbar the door or shutters to look out. The Apaches might be lurking just beyond them, waiting for her to do that very thing.

Another spasm shook her body, and a black mood enveloped her. Inexorably, she was aware of her thoughts tiptoeing toward dangerous grounds; moving back to that day almost a year ago when—

No! She fought the memory down, but it was so brutally persistent!

It was always like that.

Persistent.

Sometimes coming upon her when she least expected . . . sometimes developing slowly in spite of her strongest efforts to force it back into the dark recesses of her memory where, like a malarial infection, it forever lurked, ready to spring upon her.

Persistent!

Jane shook her head as if to dislodge the haunting nightmare and be done with it. Still, she knew it must spring forth now—it always did; an ugly vision that would torment her to her grave.

A sound startled her and the pan of water upon her lap nearly spilled to the floor. Jane Weston's head flung around and her eyes were riveted upon the front door, then upon the heavy wooden bar fitted between iron rungs.

There it was again. Footsteps scraping softly outside on the porch.

Jane shoved the pan aside and lunged for the bedroom door, gripping the jamb until her knuckles turned white, feeling her heart pounding as if any moment it must burst from her chest.

The door handle turned.

Jane sucked in a breath.

There followed a knock.

"Who is it?" she asked, still clutching the jamb.

"It's me."

At once the panic fled her. Jane rushed across the room and threw the bar off. "You've come back!"

Brandish stepped inside, refitted the bar to the door, and turned to contemplate her curiously. Jane was instantly embarrassed, for she saw the slightly humorous look that came to his eyes.

"You sound like you didn't expect me."

You're acting like a foolish child! She got a grip on her herself. "No, of course I expected you," she muttered, "It's just that I didn't expect you so soon."

He grinned and she squirmed inside. Was this man capable of seeing right through to her very soul? It had been a thinly veiled lie after all, and at once she regretted having told it. She tried to cover her sudden uneasiness with a faltering smile, and failed miserably at that as well.

"How's your husband doing?" Brandish asked, hanging his service revolver on the peg with his saber.

At least he was polite enough to pretend not to be aware of her embarrassment. Jane followed his glance to the bedroom, where a corner of the bed was just visible through the open doorway. "No change yet. But I did get him to swallow water."

Brandish dropped the lump of jerked beef he had taken from Ben Smith's saddlebags upon the table. "He's going to need something more than water soon. Ruby always kept her larders full,

Brandish

but I brought this along just the same. Perhaps you can boil some of it into a broth and we can get some food into him at the same time."

Jane glanced at the paper bundle, feeling at last the ghost that haunted her life melt back into the recesses of her memory, ready to strike again when she least expected. She tried to feign a calmness which was neither there, nor appropriate at the moment.

"Where did you find that?"

"It was among Ben Smith's things." Brandish placed the two rifles and the cartridge box on the table. "These bullets were among his effects. I found them in his saddlebags. They should give us a wider edge when the Apaches return."

"When they return? You talk like you know that they will. . . . You *do* know, don't you?" Her fingers gripped the back of the chair. "Where have you been?"

"Doing some scouting."

"For what?"

"For whatever I could find."

Damn him! Why was he being purposefully evasive now? Why doesn't he come right out and say it? Does he think this is making it any easier?

"And what was it you found, Captain Brandish?" she said evenly.

He considered her a moment, and she saw that he was measuring his words before he spoke. "There are three Apache warriors camped back in the hills behind the station," he said. "There can be only one reason for them being there, and that's to keep an eye on you until the rest of the band returns."

Even though she had expected it, this news staggered her. She found her way into a chair and for a long while said nothing. "It's true then," she said finally, shaking her head. "They are coming back. And it's me they'll be coming for!"

"That's the way I see it, ma'am." Then a thin smile arose from the frown. "Although I don't think they'll be any too selective when they do come."

"We're all as good as dead, then!" The words exploded from her. She couldn't help it. She tried to hold back her tears, but exhaustion and the ordeal of the last several days were breaking her down. Through the fog that had suddenly flooded her brain, she heard his words, and somehow the sound of them seemed to help her get a hold on her emotions.

"I wouldn't go giving us up for dead just yet," he said. There was strength in his words that she suddenly found herself able to draw from, as she had drawn from Jonathan's strength after—no, she could not permit herself to think of that now.

She wiped at her eyes and discovered they were dry. "What do you propose, Captain," she said, managing to hide the frayed and tattered other person that resided within her.

He grinned. "The first thing that I propose to do is to eat something while we have the time. Ruby always prided herself on a well-stocked pantry for the guests that the stages brought. We might as well take advantage of it now. If the

Brandish

Apaches return soon, we might not get back to it for a while."

"That's all?" she asked, irritated by the simplicity of his suggestion. She averted her eyes beneath his curious stare.

What was he looking at, anyway?

"No, that's not all. How long have you been without sleep?" he asked unexpectedly.

She glanced up. "I don't remember. Days, I should think. I might have dozed that first night with Jonathan. It's all so unclear now."

"We still have several hours of night left. After you have something to eat, go and find a blanket and get some sleep."

"But—"

"I'll see to Jonathan," he said, anticipating her objection.

"And when will you sleep?"

"Later."

Jane frowned.

"And in the morning, if we don't have any visitors, I'll see what I can do about righting that stagecoach out front."

"Why?"

"We'll need some way to get out of here."

"You'll never pull it with one horse," she said.

"Well, not very fast," he replied, "but there's no other way I can think of to get you and a wounded man to Fort Bowie, which at the moment is the nearest help I know of. If you have any other suggestions, I'm open to them."

She shook her head. "No. I have no suggestions, Captain."

Brandish took the lamp into the back room and stopped just inside the doorway, holding it high so the flickering light fell full upon Jonathan Weston's fevered face. Jane came up behind him. When Brandish turned back, furrows had deepened in the sun-darkened skin of his forehead. He seemed to be studying her again, measuring her somehow with his eyes, although his face never revealed what it was he was looking for.

He glanced at Jonathan once more, in that same careful manner, and without another word returned the lamp to the table and poured himself another cup of coffee.

"I'm not hungry," Jane said. "You eat without me." She found a blanket in the bedroom, flung it over her shoulders, and sat back at the table. Inexorably, her head lowered to her folded arms. The weight of it was suddenly too much to bear any longer. Behind her came the scrape of wood and the creak of a hinge as the shutter bar lifted and the heavy wooden planks swung open. A breeze swept in, fresh and cooling, scented with sage and sand, and the faint odor of the corrals and barns out back.

He was just standing there, staring out into the night. Looking for what? The shutter closed after a moment, the pleasant breeze at once clipped off.

She couldn't allow herself to fall asleep now. Not with him so near. But despite her mightiest efforts to keep them open, her eyelids fought against her as if they had a mind of their own, and Jane Weston was too exhausted to resist.

Brandish

"What time is it, Captain?" she asked, nuzzling deeper into the softness of her own arms, aware of a sudden, comfortable oblivion flooding into her brain.

She never did hear his reply.

Chapter Ten

A thin, pink line growing behind the hills telegraphed that morning was on the verge of blossoming. In the early chill, Ethan Brandish came off the porch, loosing the revolver in its holster at his waist, and took a careful stroll around the station. Details of the land were emerging out of the blackness of the night just past, and when he paused a moment to watch a pair of ducks leaving rippling V-shaped waves in their wake upon the still water of the pond, he knew the peacefulness of this moment could not last. With a sudden overwhelming sadness, he glanced at the blacksmith's hut.

That would have to be his first chore.

Brandish put a hand around the saber scabbard at his side to prevent it from rattling and continued his surveillance around the front of the station, stepping back up to the plank-board porch. He stomped a foot and heard the solid wood ring beneath his heal. He found it odd and completely incongruous. Where he had grown up, in Ohio on his parents' farm, if there had been wood enough to lay out a floor to walk on, it would have been put *inside* the house. Here, they had put the wood outside, on the porch, and inside the builders had made the floors out of adobe mud mixed with cow blood. As it turned out, the floors were quite substantial, easy to sweep clean, and even somewhat attractive with their reddish brown tint—but still foreign to an Eastern-bred man. Brandish wondered if he would ever get used to this Southwestern form of construction.

He studied the station. It had one thing going for it. It was sturdily built, as if designed to withstand a good many Apache attacks. It had small, deep windows with sturdy shutters. No Indian bullet would penetrate adobe walls that stood two feet thick, unlike wood. Inside, the roof was held up by fat, peeled logs—*vigas* the locals called them. And above them, peeled sticks spanned each log, arranged in a herringbone pattern. Brandish had observed the building of these types of structures during the construction of new Fort Lowell, seven miles from Tucson, and what had been old Camp Lowell. Above the sticks would be a thick layer of mud plaster, and probably several inches of stones over that.

One thing was certain, the Apaches would have a devil of a time digging through it.

The ex-captain measured the building with the eyes of a tactician. It was defensible, but not ideally located. Put in a supply of water and conserve ammunition, and they just might be able to hold out until help came. . . .

But that was a long shot, not something to bank on. Slowly his view came around and fixed upon the overturned stagecoach lying in the front yard. He tugged thoughtfully at his chin. Coarse whiskers had begun to sprout, and he knew that if he looked in a mirror, there would be more gray among them than brown.

Could the coach be lifted?

There was a way—if only the Apaches would give him enough time.

Brandish went down to the coach, gave the undercarriage a couple of shakes, bent to study the axles, frowned, kicked a steel tire, and then nodded his head. Other than a ragged canvas top, and the boot being ripped open and the luggage strewed about, the vehicle appeared sound. He pulled an arrow from the thin, poplar side panel, taking a piece of splintered wood with it, and ran a hand over the smooth lacquered surface. The coach was well constructed, and it had been finished with pride.

The Abbot-Downing Company at Concord, New Hampshire, built a coach that was designed to take the rigors of wilderness travel and still offer a measure of comfort to the passengers it carried. But comfort came at a price. In this case, the price was a weight of almost two thousand pounds.

Brandish

This particular one was a Celerity Coach, designed by Downing as a lighter, faster version of their massive Concord Coach. It was just the thing for mountain travel, and a fairly common sight in this part of Arizona Territory. The stagecoach was meant to be pulled along by six horses, but in this country they used mules. A mule could outwork a horse, and outlast it. Crook had a stable full of them at Fort Bowie, for he was a firm believer in the stout, short beasts.

Even if Brandish did manage to get the monstrous vehicle back up upon its wheels, could his one horse haul it all the way to Fort Bowie?

Brandish considered the situation in the growing light of morning. There had to be a way. His eye caught a glint of sunlight off of something beneath the driver's seat. With the toe of his boot he kicked at the dirt until he was able to free the short-barreled Parker breech-loading eight-gauge gun. In a compartment beneath the driver's seat was a box of paper shells for it.

He grinned. Their defensive capabilities at least were improving. But it still didn't solve the problem of getting Jane, Jonathan, and himself away from here to someplace safe.

Ethan Brandish squinted at the low eastern sun, shoved the shotgun shells into the pocket of his fatigue blouse, and bringing his thoughts back around to his immediate task, strode grimly to the blacksmith's hut.

He located a shovel inside, moved off a few paces, and began digging a hole.

* * *

Footsteps came up behind him and stopped. He would not have heard them if it had been an Apache, but just the same, he glanced at the gun nearby. When he came about, Jane Weston was standing there, her tangled hair falling straight around her shoulders, her arms locked firmly one into the other about her waist. The low morning sun put half her face into shadows. Her mouth was a cheerless slash from light to shadow. Well, she really did not have anything to be happy about, he decided.

"Good morning, Captain," she said. In spite of the sleep she had managed to get, her voice sounded tired, and the circles beneath her eyes seemed somehow more apparent in the morning light.

"Sleep well?"

Jane shrugged her shoulders. "No." Then she made a small smile. "Mrs. Cohen's chairs are not near as soft as her bed is, I suspect."

He grinned. "Walking around a bit should work the kinks out of your back."

Her laugh was unexpected, and for a moment another Jane Weston appeared. "It's not my back that hurts, Captain."

He found his grin widening. "Then perhaps a dip in the pond. Ruby had some of that fancy perfumed soap somewhere. I saw it once. It might do you good."

Jane shook her head. "No, I don't think so." Her apprehension came back. "Not with the Apaches about. I guess you'll just have to stay upwind of me a while longer." She looked at the mound of freshly overturned dirt that he had been patting smooth with the back of the shovel. "You've finished up here?"

"I'm done."

"You were out early."

"I couldn't sleep."

She smiled wryly. "Did you even try? Thank you for keeping an eye out while I did."

"Feel better?"

"A little."

"How's Jonathan? I checked in on him about an hour ago, gave him some water."

"No change. I just put a fresh damp cloth on his forehead."

"You know," Brandish said, easing his weight forward onto the shovel, "I'm just about half convinced he's going to make it. When a man hangs on this long, it's almost like he's willing himself to survive. If we can get the fever to break, well, your brother just might make it through."

His words seemed to bring a new hope to her face, and then all at once she realized what he had said, and the wariness of a trapped animal took its place.

"He is your brother, Miss Weston, isn't he?"

Jane Weston's face blanched. "He is my husband." A single step to widen the distance between them was all he needed to confirm the truth. "What makes you say he's not my husband?"

Brandish felt the wall go up between them. She

had dropped her guard, but now it was back, just as it had been the evening before.

He said, "For one thing, you're not wearing a wedding ring."

Jane clasped her hands, instinctively feeling the naked finger of her left hand. Panic rose in her eyes. They shifted away from his and then she said quickly, "I lost it—in the attack."

"If you did lose it, it was some time ago. Enough time to allow the skin to brown up even with the rest of your hand. And besides, there's enough resemblance in your faces for any fool to see you're brother and sister."

She began to speak.

Brandish went on ahead of her. "I don't know what it is you fear, Miss Weston, but you have nothing to fear from me."

Jane didn't speak, her eyes wide, staring, as if seeing something too horrible to bear. She turned swiftly away and hurried back into the stage station.

When she had disappeared inside, he set the shovel against the back of the blacksmith's hut, took up the shotgun, and headed for the barns.

Moving through the dusty stalls, Brandish collected the items he figured he might need. There was no lack of rope, leather bridles and reins, extra traces, pry bars, and even a handsome set of farrier tools. But not the one thing he had hoped to find. He passed through the horse barn to a second shed where hay was stored. From a pile of grass hay he freed a pitchfork and eyed the six sharp tines. Perhaps it would prove useful. He set it near the door, lifting his head toward the high ceiling.

And there it was, as he had half expected.

His view followed the rope across the ceiling and down the wall. In a moment he had unfastened the end of it and was bringing down the block and tackle. He put it across his shoulder, gathered up the ropes and reins, hammer and a pickax, carried them all out to the overturned coach, and went back for the shovel and the scattergun he'd left behind.

The sun was higher, and hot upon his dark wool blouse. He shed it and set his saber and revolver holster with it on the porch. Turning up his sleeves, Brandish leaned the gun against the coach and surveyed the hills and distant horizon for signs of the Apaches.

They were out there someplace. The three Indians he had discovered up in the hills were probably observing him from cover right now. Well, that couldn't be helped.

Brandish turned his thoughts to the coach, and walked a slow circle around it, viewing it from different angles to best determine how to proceed in lifting the thing. He was a soldier, a fighting man and a leader of men, not an engineer, but after considering the various possibilities, he knew the matter was not beyond him. Coming to a decision, he marked off three "X's" in the ground with the point of the pickax and set to work.

The sun moved across the sky. Some hours later, he looked up, blinking the sweat from his eyes, and watched Jane Weston coming across the yard.

"I've cooked something for lunch," she said.

Brandish straightened, dropped the shovel into the hole, and dragged a dirty arm across his forehead.

"And I fetched fresh water from the pond. Why don't you come in out of the sun and rest?"

He looked out at the open country that stretched away from the station. Short brown grass mixed with the blue-green sage, and the tall clumps of ocotillo and soap tree yucca. It was somewhat different vegetation from the countryside around Fort Lowell. There was no saguaro cactus here. Too high and cold in the winter for it, or perhaps too much moisture, he supposed. Brandish could hardly imagine any place in this part of the Territory where there was too much rain.

Here, a man could see for miles, be he an ex–cavalry officer or an Apache warrior. "Can't take the time right now. Got to get this done before they decide to return."

Jane instinctively hugged her waist as she had earlier that morning, looking at the work already completed. Two holes, hard-won in the tough ground. Two long fence rails, lashed together to extend their reach, resided in each hole. At their apex hung the block and tackle, and to the side, waiting its turn, lay a third set of fence rails lengthened to fifteen feet, securely lashed together with wet leather drying beneath the hot Arizona sun.

Brandish

"You look like you know what you're doing, Captain."

He grinned at her. "Pretending you know what you're doing, ma'am, is a lesson one learns early on after joining up with this man's army."

Jane laughed, shading her eyes against the harsh light. It was odd, he thought, how so simple an expression—a laugh—so dramatically changes a person's appearance. "Then at least let me bring you a glass of water."

"A glass of water would be appreciated."

Jane turned back to the station and Brandish lifted the shovel again. His arms and shoulders ached. His body cried out for sleep. But he could not stop now.

It seemed he had hardly thrust the shovel once into the rocky soil when Jane reappeared, carrying a tall glass. She was coming across the yard when suddenly she stopped, as if an invisible wall had risen across her way. The glass of water slipped from her fingers and shattered upon the ground.

She stood there, just staring at him.

Not *at* him, he realized suddenly, but *past* him.

Brandish wheeled about.

The Apaches had returned.

Chapter Eleven

"They're only looking us over," Brandish said when Jane Weston drew up beside him.

The line of Apaches came to a halt perhaps a thousand yards off—it was hard to tell for certain. If he had been an artilleryman he might have been better able to judge. They were astride their horses, watching the station, not moving any closer. They might have been painted for battle, but Brandish couldn't tell at this distance. The Apaches did not make a practice of wearing much paint. A slash or two of yellow or crimson across the cheek or forehead was about all an Apache warrior ever worried about.

"Why are they just sitting out there?"

"I suspect they're wondering about me," Brandish said.

"You?" She looked at him. "I can't imagine how

Brandish

one more person would make a difference. The number of people certainly didn't make any difference when they attacked the first time."

"That's true. But this time it's different." Brandish picked up the shovel and resumed digging the hole. Appearing, he hoped, not in the least concerned over their arrival.

"How is it any different?"

The shovel drove down and glanced off hard earth. "You see, they're thinking the same thing you did when you first saw me."

Jane combed a tangle of hair from her eyes with her fingers and glanced at the Apaches again. "They think you're still in the cavalry. So?"

"These Apaches have no way of knowing any differently, and now they're wondering what a lone soldier is doing here at this isolated stage stop. They're wondering too if we might not be the bait in a trap, and that perhaps there are fifty troops encamped nearby, waiting for them to attack."

"I should think they'll discover soon enough that you're alone."

Brandish nodded. The shovel plunged into the hole again and ricocheted off the hard ground at the bottom. His muscles bulged beneath the sweat-soaked shirt. "They'll send out scouts to look the countryside over real careful now. By tonight they'll know the truth. Might even decide to pay us a visit then."

"But Indians don't attack at night," she said.

Brandish stopped and looked at her curiously. "Where did you hear that from?"

Jane shrugged her shoulders. "It's common knowledge. Everyone knows that Indians don't attack at night."

He grinned. "Common knowledge will get you killed, ma'am. Don't believe it."

An angry scowl clouded her eyes. "Just last night you said they wouldn't attack until morning."

"True. Morning is the more likely time for an Apache to strike. But if they see a good reason to do it after dark, they won't let the time of day bother them one bit."

Her scowl disappeared and she said suddenly. "They're riding away."

"I figured they would," Brandish said, not looking up. "For the moment all their new leader wanted was to have a look at me. They'll be back." He rammed the shovel one more time. "There, that should do it." Leaning onto the shovel's long handle, he glanced at the departing Apaches, then back at Jane. "Now, I really can use that drink of water."

It was late in the day when Brandish finished his handiwork and stepped back a few dozen feet to admire it, slapping the dust from his hands and clothing. He studied the arrangement of tall spars, the block and tackle, and the ropes that he had tied around the belly of the stagecoach—in through its windows and out, underneath, in channels he'd dug.

It just might work.

All that was needed now was to harness his

Brandish

horse to the end of the rope, and with luck. . . .

Brandish grinned. Maybe he would go into engineering when he got back to the States. He'd always had an interest in mechanical things. He went back to the spars and tried to determine their strength.

A vapor of uncertainty drifted over him.

The poles had been dried to tinder in the hot Arizona climate, made brittle in the dryness; two thousand pounds might be more than they could take. He'd already scoured the coach for any unnecessary weight, and there was not an awful lot about the vehicle that could be conveniently removed, or that wasn't needed to make the thing run. He had emptied the boot, cut away what leather remained of it, and unloaded the toolbox.

There were still a few items he could yet remove. The doors could be discarded, and the seats were unnecessary now. Jonathan would travel better stretched on the floor anyway.

Movement on the horizon drew his eye. He suspected the Apaches had returned, but after a couple of minutes watching the shape grow larger, he knew differently. Brandish went back inside the stage station, and came out onto the porch with his field glasses.

"It's a buckboard. Drawn by a pair of horses, with one—no, two people on the seat." Brandish lowered the glasses and looked at Jane. "There goes a whole day's work out the window," he said, glancing at the spars and rigging he had just finished putting together in the yard.

She took the glasses from him. After a long look, she handed them back. "You almost sound disappointed."

"I am . . . almost." He grinned at her. "Sort of wanted to see if all my fancy engineering would work. But just the same, I'm more than willing to catch a ride on that buckboard and make a run for Fort Bowie before the Apaches come back."

"Will we be able to move Jonathan in his condition?" she asked.

He'd momentarily forgotten that. "I don't know. If you weigh the odds, he'll be no worse off in the back of that buckboard than in that feather bed if the Apaches breach our defenses."

The buckboard was close now. Brandish made out the driver, a woman in a wide sunbonnet, with a child in a straw hat beside her. They approached the yard and slowed, as if suddenly made wary by what they saw there. Brandish put the binoculars in Jane's hand and stepped down off the porch.

The buckboard drew to a halt beyond the overturned stagecoach. The spars and riggings looked purposeful and mighty impressive, Brandish thought as he strode out to meet her, as if someone had put a great expense of time and muscle into them. He rotated a stiffening shoulder.

The woman's dark arms lowered, the reins settled in her lap, and her head lifted. Brandish was surprised to discover a black face beneath the wide brim of the bonnet, looking at him—and he was disheartened too, for he knew why she had come. Beside her sat a young boy, his rich brown skin glistening in the sunlight.

The woman's eyes moved across his dusty uniform and at once they hardened, like shining obsidian. "Is Mr. Cohen around?" she asked in a coolly detached voice when Brandish stopped by their horses, a handsome pair of chestnuts. They were well-muscled, deep-chested draft animals, the kind that could pull a loaded-down buckboard all day and not tire.

"No, he's not. Please bring the buckboard to the station, ma'am."

She glared at him. "I'm not in the habit of takin' orders from just any man, and certainly not from one in the United States Cavalry. I'll wait for Mr. Cohen inside, and if I choose t' leave my rig right here, sir, I will do just that." She glanced around the station yard and her view settled upon the overturned coach. "What in the world happened here?"

"You're Mrs. Smith, aren't you?"

Her eyes came back to him, wary this time. "I'm Ilsa Smith. But how do you . . . ?" She looked back at the overturned coach. "Where's my husband? Where's Ben Smith?"

"Let me help you down—"

She wrenched her arm from his hand. "I do not need nor do I desire any help from the *cavalry!*" she shot back. "Where's my husband?"

"What's wrong, Mamma?" the boy said, sensing her alarm.

Ilsa Smith put a hand on his arm, but her gaze

remained fixed upon Brandish. "Where's my husband? I ain't a'gonna ask you again."

There was never an easy way to say it except straight out, and Lord knows, Ethan Brandish had had a lot of practice. "Your husband is dead, Mrs. Smith."

His words took her breath away, but the boy seemed not to immediately grasp their full meaning.

"Mamma?" His large round eyes looked up at her as if hoping she had some rational way to explain what he had just heard.

Ilsa Smith did not speak at once, but the hardness in her eyes melted as they filled with tears. "No," she said softly.

"I'm sorry," Brandish said.

She blinked. A glistening streak appeared upon her cheek and made its way down to her chin. "But he only came to deliver the mules—?" she said.

"The stage station was attacked by Apaches, ma'am. When I arrived here yesterday I found only two survivors, one badly wounded."

"Ben—?"

"No. He wasn't one of them."

"Ruby?"

Brandish shook his head.

Ilsa Smith sniffed and drew her son close, her nails digging into his shoulders. The boy had begun to cry softly as he slowly understood, trying mightily not to let the tears show.

Ethan Brandish frowned, took hold of the horses, and led them to the station.

Brandish

Jane remained on the porch a moment, as if uncertain what to do next, then she went down to Ilsa and said, "Please come inside."

Ilsa looked up, surprised to discover her standing there. She nodded her head and climbed down. Brandish took the buckboard around back, unhitched the horses, and turned them into the corral with his own mount. He pitched in some hay, made certain there was water in the trough, and when he returned to the house, Ilsa and the boy were at the table. Jane was heating water on the stove.

The handsome woman glanced up and touched her eyes dry with a handkerchief. The boy hid his face in her shoulder and she instinctively worked her fingers into his tight hair and held him close. "My husband. Where's Ben?"

"I buried him with the others."

She gathered her resolve. The news of Ben's death had hit her hard and knocked her back a step, but Ilsa Smith was made of stern stuff, and Brandish could see she had taken back control of herself. Her eyes narrowed at him and immediately a hostility which he did not understand returned.

"I see by your uniform that you're a captain," she said curtly. "I guess then your troops are out trying to run down the savages that did this?"

"I'm alone."

"Alone?" She apparently had not expected that. Ilsa sniffed back her tears. "I don't understand how this could have happened. The Indians have always been friendly to us. They used to call Ben

'Buffalo Man,' and after Crook brought in the last of Cochise's people last year we've hardly seen a single Apache about."

"Crook didn't bring them all in, ma'am. There are still some Coyoteros on the loose. One named Yellow Shirt had escaped back into the Tonto Basin, and he came back to make trouble. I only just got word of him last week. When Yellow Shirt attacked, Ben fought against him. In combat, bullets and arrows don't discriminate."

She glared sharply, "Too bad you can't say the same for the cavalry." She bit her lip and said with sudden gentleness, "Ruby and Frank were our friends. Of course Ben would have fought with them." The tears returned. "Oh, why did he have to die?"

Jane put a hand on Ilsa's shoulder. "I'm sorry," she said softly. The teapot whistled just then and Jane went to tend to it.

"Jasper," the boy said, his words muffled against her shoulder.

Ilsa patted his head soothingly.

"Where's Jasper," the boy demanded.

Ilsa looked at Brandish. "Ben had a dog with him."

"The dog is dead."

"Oh." She lowered her eyes and said nothing else.

Brandish took up the shotgun and stepped outside. He paused beneath the overhang of the porch to study the hot land beyond, not seeing any Apaches. But that meant nothing. He took a dipper of water from the olla hanging there in the shade. It was only marginally cooler than the air. Hitching the shotgun under his arm, he went around back to the corrals to check on the horses.

The buckboard's bed was long enough to take a man lying down, and there was room enough for Jane to tend to him. Brandish ran a finger around the axle hubs. They had been recently greased.

He rested a boot on the bottom rail of the corral. The animals had their heads buried in the grass hay he had pitched for them—his own mount and a matched pair of fine-looking draft horses. Ilsa Smith had a good team, Brandish decided. These two would be able to move them along at a brisk pace, and keep it up for many hours.

If they were lucky, they would be seeing the adobe barracks of Fort Bowie by dawn.

Ethan Brandish frowned suddenly, and rubbed his rough chin. Jonathan Weston would not likely survive such a trip in his condition. It would be a hell of an ordeal for even a healthy man, and one so near to death could not be expected to arrive alive. But if they remained here a day or two for the man to gain some strength, none of them would come out of this alive.

It was a hard decision, but hard decisions were what Ethan Brandish had been trained to make.

Chapter Twelve

"Here, have some tea, Mrs. Smith," Jane said, setting the cup on the table in front of the weeping woman.

Ilsa didn't take the cup at once, but touched the corner of her eye with the handkerchief and said, "It's hard to believe that Ben's dead. Only this morning everything was as it ought to be. I was doing my chores, tending the stock, and getting a little concerned about Ben being away so long, so Jamie and me, we decided to come out looking for him. But really, I wasn't all that worried. It was no more than an excuse to come visit with Ruby. Ben was often gone for days at a time. But it can get so awful lonely out here on the desert...."

Jane sat down across the table from Ilsa, cradling her own cup between her palms. But the coffee in it was cold.

Ilsa glanced up suddenly. "Tell me what happened." Her grip tightened about the boy still clinging to her side. "How did Ben die?"

The Apache raid was not something Jane cared to think back on, but she had already explained it once to Brandish, and this time it seemed to come a little easier. She stood and looked out the back window. Beyond it, Jane saw the tall ex-cavalry captain working in the corrals. She quelled a shiver and turned back to the woman and boy at the table.

"They attacked just after breakfast. My hus—" Jane caught herself. That lie was no longer necessary. Had it ever really been?

"—my brother, Jonathan—" she said, inclining her head at the bedroom door. Ilsa's glance followed it. "—was with your husband in the barn. They had gone out together to examine the mules Ben had brought by the previous evening, shortly after the stage had arrived. The mules were such sturdy, strong little animals, and Jonathan was admiring them."

Ilsa nodded and smiled proudly through her grief. "It was Ben's idea to raise mules for the stage company, and the army. Hoof stock was what he knew how to do best. It's what he did before . . . well, before the war. But that was in another life." There was suddenly heavy sadness in her voice.

"After the war, Ben and me moved out here. It

was about as far away from the life we knowed back in Georgia as we could get. Ben got ahold of some breeding stock and began raising them strong mules. He was certain there'd be a market for strong draft animals with the stage companies. Those mules sure do make light work of hauling passengers and freight."

"My family used to raise horses," Jane said. "We had a little place on the Canadian River, in the New Mexico Territory. We've never raised mules, but Jonathan was anxious to look at them, and Ben was just as anxious to show them to him."

"That would be Ben, all right," Ilsa said, "always peacock proud of his stock." Moisture fought its way back into her eyes.

Jane said, "Ben and Jonathan were together out in the barn when the Apaches struck. They came without warning, sneaking up on foot until they were almost in the yard."

She paused and stepped to the bedroom door, looking in on the unconscious man in the next room. "I remember watching Jonathan through the window once the shooting started. He came out of the barn and tried to make it back to the house. He knew we would need all the help we could get. He hadn't taken but a few steps before an Apache arrow struck him down. Your husband appeared then at Jonathan's side, like a protecting angel from God. He had his rifle, and was firing it just as fast as he could chamber the next bullet. Ben seemed to have a sense about the

Indians. Almost as if he knew instinctively where the next shot ought to go."

"Your husband managed to keep the Indians away until he could pull Jonathan back into the barn. He fought a while from there. The walls were good and thick, but it wasn't a favorable position, I suppose. There was no way for Ben to help us in here. The Indians seemed to understand that, and they were purposely drawing his fire, and keeping him pinned down back there while the others hit us hard from the front."

Jane turned away from the bedroom and studied Ilsa. The woman at the table was waging a battle of her own now. Grief was a relentless opponent. How well Jane knew that.

"The fighting went badly from the start," Jane continued. "First Mr. Waterworth—he was a tool drummer from back East. He was on the same coach as we. He was killed. Hank Cloy, the driver, he died next, and then Mr. Cohen—" Jane paused, transfixed by the recollection of the battle.

"Yes?" Ilsa prompted.

Her words brought Jane around. How long had she been back there, reliving that horror? She felt her cheeks warm beneath the other woman's intense gaze. "I'm sorry, what was I saying?"

"Mr. Cohen . . ."

"Oh yes. Mr. Cohen. After he died there was only Ruby and me. We both knew it would only be moments before the savages overran the station, and I think we both understood in some unspoken way that we would be better off dead than falling into their hands." A shiver wracked Jane's body and she hugged herself, rubbing her arms to drive away the chill.

"Ruby took the gun from Mr. Cohen's hand and went to the window. Then a bullet—" Jane stopped again and glanced at her hands. Her fingers were woven tight, and white as a bleached sheet. She unfolded them and wiped them upon her blouse as if to remove something foul and ugly. "Mrs. Cohen was suddenly in my arms and bleeding, and, well, it all sort of becomes unclear after that."

Jane looked up sharply, with wide eyes that bore deep into Ilsa. "He knew somehow—your husband, Ben. He knew that he had to get back to the house. Suddenly I heard renewed gunfire coming from the barn, and when I sprang to the window, Ben had just made a break for the station."

Jane's eyes filled with admiration and sorrow.

"He was magnificent, Mrs. Smith, coming across the yard with only his rifle to keep the savages at bay, firing as swiftly as it took for him to work the lever and chamber the next bullet.

"The Apaches fell back. They couldn't get near Ben. He had an instinct about them, turning and swinging that rifle as if it was divinely guided. And that wonderful dog, always right there at his side, growling and snapping out, not leaving him."

Ilsa Smith smiled faintly through her tears. "It would be just like Ben to take on the whole

Brandish

Apache war party. He never could fully shed that part of his life. Every time he saw a man in uniform it gnawed at him, like a bad case of the gout."

"Your husband was in the military?"

"It's not important, Miss Weston. Another life, that's all . . . another cross folks like Ben and me have to bear. Please, tell me what happened next."

Jane frowned. She stood and went to the stove for a fresh cup of coffee. "Would you like some?"

"No, thank you. My tea is fine."

Jane sat back down, and after a moment she rolled her shoulders as if shifting a heavy weight, and said, "It was a valiant attempt, but in the end . . ." She discovered that she did not want to finish the sentence, but Ilsa Smith wanted to know how her husband had died. Jane straightened in the chair and said, "Ben would have made it to the station had he not run out of bullets. I'm certain of that. I watched him frantically attempting to reload the rifle, and there was nothing I could do to help. They swarmed down on him and poor Mr. Smith didn't have a prayer."

The boy was crying openly now, and so was his mother. They had lost so much, and she could not help but wonder why she and her brother had survived it all. She winced inwardly at a sharp pang of guilt. The others had been sacrificed for their sake! Jane knew it was a foolish notion, yet just the same, the guilt lingered on.

She stood. "Well, I better be getting some supplies together. I'm sure Captain Brandish will be wanting to leave soon."

"What's *he* doing here?" Ilsa Smith asked sharply. Jane was momentarily taken aback by the bitterness she heard in the woman's voice.

"Captain Brandish? I'm not altogether certain. I gathered he intended to pay a visit to the Cohens. They had been friends, and Captain Brandish was on his way back East. He arrived a day after the attack."

"Back East? But what happened to his men?"

"He has none with him." Jane was about to say that Brandish was no longer in the cavalry, but she decided that was his business, and his place to tell.

Something changed in Ilsa's eyes. "Why's he alone? Why isn't the army out chasing down the Indians who attacked the station?"

"I wondered that too, at first."

"Odd," Ilsa said softly, as if to herself.

"What?"

"An army captain riding out alone in this country, unescorted. He ought to have known better."

"I'm sure I don't know what Captain Brandish's reasons are, Mrs. Smith." Jane cared not to pursue the course of Ethan Brandish's private affairs. "I have no understanding of how the military operates."

Ilsa Smith gave a short laugh, her bitterness again apparent. "Well, I certainly understand the military all too well, Miss Weston," and she stood out of her chair. "Allow me to help you. The work will be good for me."

Brandish

"You don't have to—"

"I know I don't have to. I want to. I need to." Ilsa Smith said to her son, "You stay here, Jamie."

"Yes, Mamma," he said, rubbing away a tear.

There was a strength in the two of them, Jane thought, a strength that they drew from each other. Like she and her brother—like she and Cap—

Jane immediately dismissed that notion before it had a chance to take root. It was only she and Jonathan, and that was the way it was going to have to be from now on. She could never again trust another man. Not after—No! She mustn't permit herself to remember. Not now, when so much needed to be done.

Ilsa's hand rested momentarily on Jamie's shoulder, then she turned away, dabbed her eyes, and joined Jane in the back room, where Jonathan Weston lay, still unconscious.

Chapter Thirteen

Ethan Brandish came around the back of the stage station and drew suddenly to a halt. He shaded his eyes against the lowering sun and his view narrowed at the line of riders that had appeared in the distance.

The Apaches were back.

He smiled to himself. It hadn't taken long for them to ascertain that he was alone, but for the moment they seemed in no hurry to move on the station, content to keep a safe distance—for a while at least—to discourage exchange of gunfire.

Still looking me over.

He climbed the steps to the porch and went inside the station. Jane glanced over from the cupboard where she was transferring Ruby's

Brandish

canned goods into an open pillowcase. "I'm almost ready here," she said.

Ilsa was by the stove, removing a heavy pot of boiling water. At Brandish's appearance, she set it back upon the stove top and folded her arms defiantly, her face pinched in a scowl. "I don't know what you're planning, Captain," she said, "but if you expect that my wagon and my horses are going to carry you to Fort Bowie, well you just better think again. It looks to me like you made great strides toward putting that stagecoach up on its wheels, and I suggest you get back to it. I'll allow you the use of my animals for that—and only that."

Jane stopped filling the pillowcase and stared at her in silent confusion. "But we need your wagon to get to safety," she said.

"I need it too. I'm going to return to my home."

"You can't hope to return now. Not with those savages running wild."

"They never bothered me or mine before. The only reason Ben was killed was because he was helping defend this place. He put too much of himself into our home for me to abandon it now. No. For Ben's sake, I'm going back."

"You can't do that," Brandish said. The finality in his voice brought Ilsa's head around with a snap, and the smoldering fire in her dark eyes flamed.

Brandish closed the door and slid the bar in place.

Ilsa watched him, seething; her eyes narrowed

further and her nostrils flared. "Is the cavalry now in the practice of taking civilians prisoners if they don't permit them to commandeer private property?"

"Not that I'm aware of, ma'am," Brandish said, taking his Springfield to the front window.

"Then I intend to leave. Right now."

"But you can't. Please, Mrs. Smith, we need to get away from here, to get Jonathan to a doctor. Your wagon is our only hope," Jane implored.

"I am truly sorry, but I cannot help you, Miss Weston." Ilsa looked back at Brandish, her eyes dark and stormy, and remembering. "I stopped giving to the cavalry a long time ago, and I'm not gonna start now." Ilsa Smith caught Jamie by the sleeve. "Let's be on our way."

Ethan Brandish stepped in front of the door.

Ilsa reared back and ran him through with a stare. "You move aside, mister."

"I'm not going to hold you here, Mrs. Smith," he said evenly, "but before you step outside you best have a look through that window."

Ilsa considered him a moment, and in that moment Jane suddenly knew what had happened, and the expression on her face instantly changed from worry to panic.

Ilsa glared at him suspiciously, then went to the window. She grabbed the boy away from it when she discovered him standing there beside her, a sudden panic widening her black eyes.

"They've come back!"

Brandish nodded his head. "I've been expecting them."

Brandish

Fear had frozen Jane to the very spot on which she had been standing.

"Ma'am? ... Miss Weston." The firmness of Brandish's voice brought her out of her trance. "Please go into the bedroom and close and bar the shutters there." He knew to have something to do—anything—was what she needed at the moment. Fear can paralyze even the strongest person if it is not diverted immediately. In battle, Brandish had seen brave men succumb to its stranglehold. It was vital, he knew, not to allow them to think too long about an impending battle.

Jane hurried into the back room. Brandish wheeled around to Ilsa. "Perhaps in the past the Apaches have not bothered you or yours, ma'am; however, these are not Chiricahua, but Coyoteros, and if you attempt to leave this station now, I doubt you'll make it a hundred yards. Not with those Apaches intending to even up a score on this place."

Ilsa did not fully understand that, but he didn't have time to explain it all to her at the moment.

"What can I do to help, Captain?" Ilsa asked. In the face of this immediate danger, she seemed to put aside whatever grudge she held against the cavalry.

The boy had struggled free of her grip. Brandish took notice of Ilsa's son now for the first time. It was the soldier in him, he decided, suddenly confronted with overwhelming numbers, taking stock of the resources at his command. Jamie Smith was perhaps twelve years old—Not a big boy for his age. If anything, he was small. Hair cropped short, big eyes, smooth skin. There was a hint about him of the man Brandish had buried that morning, but as he studied the lad closer, it was clear that Jamie Smith favored his mother's side of the family. Still, he was only a boy, and he would need to be kept out of harm's way once the shooting began.

Brandish returned his gaze to Ilsa and put the Winchester in her hands. "This was Ben's rifle. You know how to use it?"

"Fair enough," she said. Ilsa Smith was a confident woman, and Ethan Brandish admired that.

He nodded toward the back window. "Take a position there, where you'll have a clear view of the corrals. When the Apaches attack, those horses will be one of their first targets, and we can't afford to lose them."

"I understand."

"Jamie."

The boy turned from Ilsa's side. "Sir?"

Brandish went down on his haunches, eyes level with the boy's. "I'm going to need your help too. Think you're up to it?"

Ilsa was watching Brandish with a suspicious frown.

"I don't know." Jamie looked back at his mother, but Ilsa's eyes were fixed upon Brandish.

"We got us a wounded man back in the bedroom. I need someone in there with him, to watch out that no Indians break into the room. Think you can do that for me?" There was little

Brandish

chance that the Apaches could come through those thick shutters with their heavy cross bars keeping them secure against the attack, and back there Jamie would be safe from stray bullets.

Jamie gave his mother another glance and Brandish noted the almost imperceptible nod of Ilsa's head. "Yes, I can do that," he replied, with the same confidence Brandish had observed in his mother, although his wide eyes told another story.

"Good. Go take your station."

Jamie hurried into the back room.

When Brandish looked up, something had changed in Ilsa's face. She understood what he had done, and she said, "Thank you, Captain, for putting Jamie out of the line of fire."

From the front window, Jane's panicky voice rang out. "Captain, they're coming!"

Brandish grabbed the shotgun, handed it to Jane, and spilled the box of shotgun shells into a porcelain washbasin on the floor at her side. "Hold fire until I give the word."

The Apaches rode forward and stopped at the far edge of the yard. One of them, the new leader, Brandish presumed, broke away from the rest and came forward a few paces. He reined to a stop and curiously eyed the overturned stagecoach, the spars, ropes, and tackle Brandish had erected around it.

A smile fleetingly touched the man's dark, leathery face, then it was gone, and he came forward again, drawing to a halt in front of the stage station.

"Blue soldier inside," he said, sitting erect, his long war lance held across his horse's shoulders. The warrior wore a bandolier of rifle cartridges across his chest, but he carried no rifle. Leaving the weapon behind was an act of bravado, and a test of Brandish's courage. He must have been a powerful leader, for Brandish knew there were few cartridge-firing rifles among the Indians, and to own one, and the bullets that went along with it, was a mark of distinction indeed.

"What is he up to?" Jane asked.

Brandish set his rifle aside. "It appears he wants to talk."

"You aren't going out there?"

Brandish lifted away the bar across the door. "Let's see what he wants." He unbuckled his holster belt.

"You can't go out there without a gun!"

"He came without one," Brandish said. "We wouldn't want the Apaches to think we were any less brave then they. And besides, they're not ready to attack again . . . not just yet at least."

"How can you know that?"

"When they do, you won't see them coming, and you certainly won't see them atop a horse, where they make such fine targets. No, when they attack again, Miss Weston, it will be like the first time. You won't know it until it happens."

Brandish pulled the door open. The Indian's dark eyes shifted and followed him across the porch, his face hiding the thoughts behind it.

Brandish stopped and casually, but with obvious meaning, rested a hand on the pommel of the saber at his side. His years of duty in Arizona had taught him that the Apaches respected bravery above all else.

They were not flamboyant warriors, not like the Comanches or the Shoshones. When it came time to make war they did not go in for much painting of their faces, but preferred to remain a dull, colorless people—like the land they occupied. All the easier to blend in—like the coyote and mountain lion. And like the land, the coyote, and the mountain lion, they were tough as hornstone and practically undefeatable. The Apaches stole horses not because they liked horses, but because horses were useful beasts. They cared little for the animals, unlike the Nez Percés, who practically made a living out of raising and trading horses. The Apaches seldom used the horse in battle, often preferring to eat him rather than to ride him.

"*Buenas tardes*, Captain," the Apache said, noting Brandish's uniform. "You are alone here?"

"*Buenas tardes*," Brandish replied, matching the Apache's dignified manner. "My men will be coming back soon," he lied.

The Apache grinned, showing a row of crooked teeth, worn uneven from the grit of the land. He shook his head and said, "No blue soldiers come this way. They all ride north to Apache Pass where Crook is. They leave Camp Lowell two mornings ago."

That could have been none other than McGrath and the new captain, Benton Ross. Brandish did not permit his frown to show, but it was beginning to look as if he just might miss that last drink with his old first sergeant after all. He said, "The blue soldiers are going to Fort Bowie to talk with Crook. Then they will come here and take you and your warriors to the reservation where Cochise and your brothers are."

The Apache spit at the ground, and the war lance in his fist lowered. Its chipped point halted a half foot from Brandish's chest. The ex–cavalry man did not move, but out of the corner of his eye he saw a dull glint of sunlight off of burnished steel by the window at his back. He prayed that the nervous woman behind the trigger of the shotgun would not attempt anything now. The Apache noted it too, but his full attention remained on Brandish.

Brandish said, "You called me out here to talk. What is it you want to say to me?"

"Cochise is old man. He die pretty soon. Then Rock That Sparks will be leader of all the free Apache. He will never lead his people onto the white man's reservation," the Indian said, his black eyes hard and shining.

"Are you Rock That Sparks?"

The warrior nodded his head.

"If you refuse the reservation, Crook and his soldiers will push you like the buffalo over a cliff, and no warrior of Rock That Sparks will have grandchildren to teach the old ways to. Crook has the blessings of Grant, the Great Father in Washington. This you cannot stop from happening. But you and your people can move to the reservation where you and your warriors

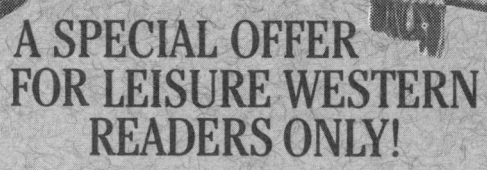

A SPECIAL OFFER FOR LEISURE WESTERN READERS ONLY!

Get FOUR FREE Western Novels

Travel to the Old West in all its glory and drama—without leaving your home!

Plus, you'll save between $3.00 and $6.00 every time you buy!

EXPERIENCE THE ADVENTURE AND THE DRAMA OF THE OLD WEST WITH THE GREATEST WESTERNS ON THE MARKET TODAY...FROM LEISURE BOOKS

As a home subscriber to the Leisure Western Book Club, you'll enjoy the most exciting new voices of the Old West, plus classic works by the masters in new paperback editions. Every month Leisure Books brings you the best in Western fiction, from Spur-Award-winning, quality authors. Upcoming book club releases include new-to-paperback novels by such great writers as:

Max Brand   Robert J. Conley   Gary McCarthy   Judy Alter
Frank Roderus   Douglas Savage   G. Clifton Wisler
David Robbins   Douglas Hirt

as well as long out-of-print classics by legendary authors like:

Will Henry   T. V. Olsen   Gordon D. Shirreffs

Each Leisure Western breathes life into the cowboys, the gunfighters, the homesteaders, the mountain men and the Indians who fought to survive in the vast frontier. Discover for yourself the excitement, the power and the beauty that have been enthralling readers each and every month.

SAVE BETWEEN $3.00 AND $6.00 EACH TIME YOU BUY!

Each month, the Leisure Western Book Club brings you four terrific titles from Leisure Books, America's leading publisher of Western fiction. EACH PACKAGE WILL SAVE YOU BETWEEN $3.00 AND $6.00 FROM THE BOOKSTORE PRICE! And you'll never miss a new title with our convenient home delivery service.

Here's how it works. Each package will carry a FREE 10-DAY EXAMINATION privilege. At the end of that time, if you decide to keep your books, simply pay the low invoice price of $13.44, no shipping or handling charges added. HOME DELIVERY IS ALWAYS FREE. With this price it's like getting one book free every month.

AND YOUR FIRST FOUR-BOOK SHIPMENT IS TOTALLY FREE!
IT'S A BARGAIN YOU CAN'T BEAT!

LEISURE BOOKS A Division of Dorchester Publishing Co., Inc.

GET YOUR 4 FREE BOOKS NOW—
A VALUE BETWEEN $16 AND $20

Mail the Free Book Certificate Today!

FREE BOOKS CERTIFICATE!

YES! I want to subscribe to the Leisure Western Book Club. Please send my 4 FREE BOOKS. Then, each month, I'll receive the four newest Leisure Western Selections to preview FREE for 10 days. If I decide to keep them, I will pay the Special Members Only discounted price of just $3.36 each, a total of $13.44. This saves me between $3 and $6 off the bookstore price. There are no shipping, handling or other charges. There is no minimum number of books I must buy and I may cancel the program at any time. In any case, the 4 FREE BOOKS are mine to keep—at a value of between $17 and $20! Offer valid only in the USA.

Name_____

Address_____

City_____ State_____

Zip_____ Phone_____

Biggest Savings Offer!

For those of you who would like to pay us in advance by check or credit card—we've got an even bigger savings in mind. Interested? Check here. ☐

If under 18, parent or guardian must sign.
Terms, prices and conditions subject to change. Subscription subject to acceptance. Leisure Books reserves the right to reject any order or cancel any subscription.

GET FOUR BOOKS TOTALLY *FREE*—A VALUE BETWEEN $16 AND $20

PLEASE RUSH MY FOUR FREE BOOKS TO ME RIGHT AWAY!

Leisure Western Book Club
P.O. Box 6613
Edison, NJ 08818-6613

AFFIX STAMP HERE

▼ Tear here and mail your FREE book card today! ▼

will have many grandchildren. My men will be coming back soon, and they will take you to the reservation."

Rock That Sparks straightened on his horse and slowly returned the war lance to his naked knees. "Many blue soldiers will die."

"Perhaps," Brandish said easily. This was not the time to show trepidation. "But for every blue soldier that you kill, two more will be sent by the Great Father to avenge him. No Apache outside of the reservation will live. This is his order. Now, tell me what it is you want here."

The Apache's head inclined toward the stage station and his long black hair with an eagle's feather woven into it slid across the back of a worn muslin shirt. "I want the woman with yellow hair. Give me the woman and we will not hurt you or Raven Woman and her son."

So, he knew about Ilsa and Jamie too. Brandish said, "I will not give you the woman with the yellow hair."

Rock That Spark's grip tightened on the war lance. "Then you will all die."

Brandish nodded his head. "If need be, we will all die."

Rock That Sparks wheeled his horse around and rode back to the warriors. They talked a moment, then heeled their horses and left in a cloud of red dust. Slowly, the faint wind dispersed it across the yard, and when Brandish turned back, Ilsa Smith was standing in the doorway, holding her husband's Winchester.

She stepped out onto the porch, moved past

him to the corner where she could see the pond, and carefully surveyed the land beyond it. "I counted twenty-three on horseback, Captain," she said, staring out across the still water.

"Yes. I did too."

Ilsa lowered the hammer on the Winchester and turned back to face him. "They didn't make any attempt at the horses, but I did catch a glimpse of at least two Apaches working their way into the hills behind the barns."

"It's the horses they'll try for next, and then they'll be coming for Miss Weston."

Ilsa suddenly came forward and stopped three feet from him, her fingers tightening around the rifle. "You heard him. They're willing to let us go. I have an eleven-year-old son in there. All you have to do—" Ilsa bit back her words and slowly shook her head. "No, of course you can't do that. I wouldn't expect you to, Captain."

Brandish took the rifle gently from her grasp and set it into the crook of his arm. "Ben thought these people important enough to die for them."

Ilsa looked up. Her tears had returned. "Ben was like that, Captain. Ben always gave and gave, and asked nothing for himself in return." The bitterness was suddenly back in her voice. "And nothing was ever given to him, either."

Ilsa gathered up her skirts and hurried back inside the station.

Brandish watched her a moment before returning his attention to the settling cloud of dust in the distance. Escape would be impossible now. It was time to start thinking like the tactician he had been trained to be.

Rock That Sparks would not waste time; he could not take a chance that Brandish's men really were returning to the stage station. No, Ethan Brandish knew the Apaches' attack would come swiftly now, and when it did, he must be prepared.

He glanced again out into the late afternoon, then up at the low sun.

Tonight, he thought, and went back inside.

Chapter Fourteen

With the flaring wick turned up, the lamp made a suitably smoky flame. Ethan Brandish drew his saber from its metal scabbard and eyed the gleam of polished steel in the light. The government contracted with several companies to produce these fine sabers. This one had been made by Wilkerson, and it was the finest the military could buy.

How ironic, he thought, that in a day when congress was financially strangling the army to death, and reducing its size, even limiting the number of rounds of ammunition it allowed its soldiers to use in training, congress was still authorizing the purchase of Wilkerson sabers! He smiled slightly at the thought, and slowly pulled the blade through the smoky flame.

"What are you doin', sir?"

Brandish

Brandish glanced over. The boy's wide eyes were fixed upon the saber. "I'm making it dark."

Jamie found a bit of humor in that, in spite of his grief, and said, "Mean like me?"

He grinned. "Well, I reckon a little. I'm taking the gleam off the blade."

"Why?"

"So the moonlight won't pick it out."

"You going out to fight them Injuns with it?"

The ex–cavalry officer's mouth took a grim set and he nodded his head. "I'm going out. I hope I don't have to fight the Apaches, but a good soldier always has contingency plans."

"What's that?"

"Contingency? It means to make plans for any possible events."

"You learned that in the cavalry?"

Brandish gave the boy a grin. "Partly. But mostly you learn it just by living."

The brightness left Jamie's eyes. Brandish knew he was thinking of his father again. "My papa . . . he was in the cavalry."

"Was he, now?"

"Yes, sir. He was a sergeant." For an instant the boy seemed to stand a little taller. Then the weight of his grief drove him back down.

"The Ninth or Tenth?" Brandish asked.

"The Ninth, sir."

"He served under Ed Hatch, then."

The boy shrugged his shoulders. "I don't know."

"Colonel Hatch is a good man. He has first-class troops under him. Mostly longtime veterans. Why did your father leave?"

The boy was about to speak when his mother's voice called to him. "Jamie, come away from there."

Ilsa Smith was standing in the bedroom doorway, with anger in her dark eyes. Hesitantly, Jamie left the table. Ilsa drew him suffocatingly close. "Our business is none of yours, Captain."

"Jamie was just telling me about his father. Says he served in the Ninth Cavalry. I say that's something to be rightly proud of."

Ilsa did not answer that and instead said stiffly, "It appears that Mr. Weston's fever has broken."

"Has it?" Brandish set the saber aside. At Jonathan Weston's sickbed, he put a hand upon the man's forehead. "It has indeed broken." He glanced at Jane, who was watching him hopefully. "I must admit, I didn't expect your brother to make it, but right now my money is on him pulling through this."

"That is, if the Apaches don't kill us all first," Ilsa said at his back.

Brandish studied the woman's dark face, its hard features picked out by the low flame of the lamp on the night table. He frowned and stepped past her, back into the main room.

Jamie was standing by the stove, his eyes fixed on the long, curved blade on the table.

"You'd like to have one of these, wouldn't you," Brandish said, returning to the task of blackening the blade.

Brandish

The boy's eyes shot past him to the bedroom doorway where Ilsa stood, scowling. Jamie's expression changed, and when he looked back at Brandish he said unhappily, "No sir. I guess I wouldn't want one." He glanced at the floor, shoved his hands into his trouser pockets, and leaned against the wall, staring at the stack of wood by the stove.

Brandish finished darkening the blade, and went back to the bedroom. "I'll be outside for a while, Miss Weston," he told her. "Make sure you bar the door after me. I'll identify myself when I return. Don't open the door until then, no matter what you hear."

"You're going out?" Instant panic was in her voice.

"You'll be all right in here." He tried to sound encouraging. "Keep giving your brother the broth. Now that the fever's broken I wouldn't be surprised to find him gaining consciousness soon, and when he does, he'll be hungry."

"I'll take care of him." Jane stood to walk to Brandish, but at the last minute she caught herself and stopped a comfortable distance from him. "You take care of yourself, Captain Brandish."

"I will, ma'am." He wondered if her concern was genuinely for him, or if it was only that she was terrified at the thought of being left unprotected again. He buttoned up his blue fatigue blouse and buckled his holster belt over it. When he opened the door, the refreshing chill of the night air momentarily swept into the stuffy room. Brandish took a quick look along the porch, and slipped outside.

He pressed up against the adobe wall of the station, where the shadows were deep, and stayed there until he heard the bar slide heavily back in place on the other side of the door.

The undisturbed sounds of crickets and toads down by the pond was reassuring. Moonlight was a gray shine off the still water there, almost as bright as a lantern, and he made a note that that would be a place to avoid as he moved out, keeping to the shadows where he was able, and when he was not, sprinting swiftly and pulling up silently to wait long, painstaking minutes.

The Apaches were patient warriors, like a cat mounting a vigil at a mouse hole, and Brandish could afford to be no less so.

When the night's stillness remained unbroken, he moved out again. Finding a position at the corner of the barn where the moonlight did not reach, Brandish hunkered down against the cool adobe wall and rested the long, darkened blade of his saber across his knees. The horses in the corral nearby caught his scent and threw their heads nervously, but his was a familiar smell, and after a few moments they settled back down into a light sleep.

The night drew on, and the desert chill deepened, working its way through the heavy wool of his uniform blouse.

The moon arced overhead.

His knees and legs cramped. He shifted his

weight and tried not to doze. The songs of the insects were both hypnotic and reassuring. The fatigue of the last couple of days began to weigh upon him. It had been almost two days since his last real sleep.

Brandish resisted the urge to shut his eyes—if only for a few minutes—and he fell into a long-practiced routine of standing watch, a part of his brain alert and riveted on every sound, odor, and shifting shadow, while another part occupied itself with other matters.

He thought of Sergeant McGrath.

Brandish had known McGrath for three years. The stocky sergeant was a seasoned veteran who had taken to army life like he'd been born and bred to it—like Ben Smith's mules had been born and bred to the harness. As far as Brandish could recall, the discomforts of long weeks in the saddle or on foot had never once fazed the tough little sergeant. So long as he knew that at the end of the patrol there would be a warm barrack, a firm army bed, and a post-trader's store nearby with a supply of whiskey available—and, of course, a camp commander that didn't prohibit his men from indulging—McGrath was content.

Even now, at this late hour, Ethan Brandish figured his ex–first sergeant would be at the post-trader's place at Fort Bowie, an elbow on the bar, a mug in his fist. He would probably be laughing it up with the other enlisted men, and either praising the new captain, Benton Ross, or cussing him, depending on how that first patrol had gone.

McGrath would have expected Brandish to be at Fort Bowie by now, and come the morrow, or the next, if he didn't show up, McGrath would begin to get concerned. After a while, McGrath would try to talk Benton Ross into taking a patrol to the stage station to find out what had happened to him.

Brandish frowned into the night where he hunkered among the shadows that hid him, wondering how long it would take for McGrath to convince someone to come looking for him. If it took too long, all they'd be liable to find would be more bodies to bury.

The sounds of singing crickets suddenly ceased. Brandish came instantly alert. The horses in the corral continued to sleep undisturbed, but Brandish knew something had moved out in the darkness. He tightened his grip upon the pommel of his saber and worked the cold from his fingers. He briefly considered the revolver at his side, but dismissed that idea. There was no telling how many Apaches there might be nearby, and the sound of the revolver going off would bring them all down on him at once. And besides, there was only so much ammunition left. The saber did not expend bullets.

The horses came out of their sleep then, snorted and began to trot around the perimeter of the corrals, heads high, sampling the wind. In the moonlight, something gray moved, and then it was gone. Brandish's eyes focused on the slop-

Brandish

ing ground at the rear of the corrals, where he had seen movement. It was not so very far from the shadowy corner of the barn where he was crouched.

The first Apache appeared like a ghost, emerging soundlessly from the night, stealing silently across the open ground to the corral. He stopped to scout around. Moonlight touched his face a moment before he slipped under the bottom rail.

The horses whinnied softly and bunched at the far side of the corral. There had to be at least one more Apache nearby, Brandish was certain, but he could not detect him immediately, and he knew he would never spot the Indian until the warrior made a move. By then, it would be too late. The horses would be gone, and with them any hope for escape.

The Apache in the corral had his back to him. Brandish took the opportunity to slip out of cover. In an instant he was under the bottom rail. The nervous sounds of the horses covered his footsteps until he was almost upon him . . .

And then a voice cried from somewhere in the darkness.

The Apache spun around in a crouch, with gray light glinting off of something in his fist. The warrior sprang like a bobcat. At the same instant, Brandish caught a glimpse out of the corner of his eye of movement beyond the corral poles.

A second Apache had been nearby all along.

In the moonlight, the Apache's short blade moved in a arc. Brandish dodged aside and brought the saber up and forward in a lunge. It hit something hard, then sank deep. A short, strangled cry rang out, the weight of a sinking body dragged the saber down.

Brandish had lost sight of the second Apache, but instinctively he knew where he would find him. With a mighty pull, Brandish freed the point of the saber from the breastbone of the first Apache and swung around.

The tip of the war lance was but inches from his back, and the slashing sword sheared it off two feet short.

Ethan Brandish came full about and lunged. The second Indian leaped lightly aside with the shortened shaft of the lance still clutched in his hands.

He swung it at the soldier.

Brandish heard it slice the air above his head, and once again he lunged forward. As he did so, he suddenly had a vision of the tall, slender instructor at Fort Riley who wore a monocle when he wasn't teaching soldiers the fine art of saber combat.

"It is a gentleman's veapon," Sergeant von Kliner had said often, his words carrying a thick German accent. Brandish heard them clearly again, as if the old Prussian instructor was even now at his side. Rumor had it that von Kliner was of an aristocratic background, but had to flee Germany, and the emperor's soldiers, because of an affair of the heart with a member of Frederick William's family. But von Kliner never spoke of his past.

Even back then—almost twenty years now—

Brandish

the notion of swords and sword fighting seemed archaic to Brandish. It was, after all, the day of revolvers, the rifle, and long-range artillery. Just the same, he had been smitten with the idea of learning the use of a weapon that had served so well for thousands of years. At the time, he recalled thinking that the whole notion of edged warfare was somehow foreign, European in its flair, and the fancy footwork involved in the use of a saber something better worked out on a dance floor—preferably with a lovely young woman in your arms—than on a battlefield. But Brandish had been a serious student, and he had learned.

Now the techniques von Kliner had drummed into his head came back to him. Brandish had never seriously used the saber in combat, but that didn't seem to matter as he parried the spear shaft that drove in at him. His riposte came effortlessly, and it set the Indian stumbling back. He clearly had not expected that.

Steel and wood clashed.

The Apache tried again, but this sort of lunge and parry combat was not the Indian's natural way of fighting, and with sudden frustration, he flung the useless stick away, drawing his own short knife like a cat bares its claws. At once, a grim line eased across the Apache's face. With the knife, he was fighting on his own terms.

But a knife was no match for a saber in trained hands.

Brandish easily parried the first attack, aware that he must make short work of this battle, for he had no way of knowing if another Apache even now was advancing on his unprotected rear flank.

Brandish feinted to the right, and as the Apache dodged left, Brandish executed an immediate flèche in that direction. The sudden reversal caught the Indian off guard, and before he could recover, the point of Brandish's saber had plunged deep into hard abdominal muscle and ran on through the stomach, stopping firmly at the man's spine.

His momentum drove the Indian back half a dozen feet. Wide, dark eyes stared unbelievingly at him, and then down at the length of steel, before turning up in death.

Brandish freed his weapon and came about, ready for the next Apache, but except for the nervous gathering of horses at the far end of the corral, the night remained silent. Knowing it was dangerous to linger in the moonlight any longer than necessary, Brandish merged once again with the shadows, and crouched behind a mesquite hummock a few hundred feet off to wait, hearing the rasping sound of his own breath, feeling the gradual retreat of his heartbeat.

After a while, the horses settled down, and finally the sounds of crickets returned.

Brandish drew in a long, quiet breath, let it out slowly, and only then did he dare to remove his watch and see what hour it was.

Almost two o'clock.

Brandish

He tucked the watch back into his pocket, and once again keeping to the shadows, moved off into the surrounding hills, away from the stage station.

Chapter Fifteen

He knew the way this time, and traveled swiftly through the darkness, careful to remain as silent as the enemy he now sought. As Brandish moved higher into the hills behind the stage station, he was aware of a heaviness in his heart that he did not quite understand. He thought of the Apache soldiers back at Forts Lowell and Bowie that Crook had hired to track down their own people, and of the men, women, and children bunched together in places like the Chiricahua reservation, or Camp Verde.

For the most part, the Apaches were friendly and obliging people. There were, however, always those few renegades—like the two men lying dead in the corral back at the stage station.

The enemy.

Brandish did not consider the Apaches his en-

Brandish

emy. Perhaps it was that. They were an adversary to be sure, and a deadly one, but were they his enemy? Brandish wondered if history had turned out differently, and it was he defending his home against an unstoppable tide of invading foreigners, would he be so much different than Cochise, or Mangas Coloradas—or Rock That Sparks?

Who was the enemy?

Brandish had grown to respect and admire the Apaches; had become friends with the Apache soldiers and scouts at the fort, and of late had grown to resent having to kill such a brave and valiant people. Yet while he wore the uniform of the United States Cavalry, the Apaches must remain his enemy until every last one had been defeated and moved onto the reservation, and there was little he could do to change that.

Had that been the reason all along why he had resigned his commission? The thought startled him and brought him to a halt. Fortunately, he didn't have to deal with this new, troubling question for long. He had arrived at the place that he'd discovered the night before.

The odor of wood smoke was thick in the air, and the sound of voices—words chanted rather than spoken—reached him from beyond the next low ridge.

If Rock That Sparks had posted guards, Brandish did not encounter them as he crawled up to the edge of the narrow valley and peered over. Three campfires burned in the little declivity beyond, a dozen or so sleeping bodies formed dark lumps upon the land. By one of the fires sat Rock

That Sparks. The flames had burned low and their feeble light played across the Indian leader's face as he stared into them. To either side of him sat a warrior, each chanting a low song that was passed and taken up by the other. Rock That Sparks took no part in this, but instead his gaze remained steady, as if within those flames he was able to view the future—or the past.

The other two fires were encircled by a small number of Indians, talking quietly among themselves, and taking advantage of the heat; no doubt making plans for the next day.

After taking count, Brandish found the camp short seven men from the band that had showed up earlier at the stage station.

He frowned. Had five others gone looking for the two now lying dead in the corral down by the station? The ex-captain's view shifted to a crude brush corral the Indians had built a little way from the camp. Two more warriors were standing guard there. That still left them three men shy by his reckoning.

But that didn't necessarily mean anything. Brandish knew well enough that before a battle some warriors preferred to go off by themselves.

He glanced at the brush corral, and the horses dozing there, and as he eased down off the ridge line and made his way back to the stage station, the germ of a plan had been planted. He now only needed to work out the details.

* * *

Brandish

Brandish dragged the bodies of the two Apaches from the corral and left them behind the blacksmith's hut. The little burial site was becoming well populated, he mused, brushing his hands and looking out across the pond. The moon had set, and the lack of light was just one less thing to worry about. He glanced to the east. Morning was only a couple of hours off, and when it came, he expected it would be a busy one.

Brandish was aware of his immense fatigue. Now that he was no longer waiting in hiding for the Apaches, his weariness swept over him like a warm, heavy blanket. How long had it been since his last sleep? Almost two days? He crossed the dark yard to the station and knocked on the door with the pommel of his saber.

"Who's there?" came a wary reply from beyond it.

"It's me."

"Captain Brandish?" The bar slid out of its iron anchors and the door opened. Ilsa's dark face and wide eyes looked out at him. "It *is* you. You alone?"

He grinned and stepped inside. "As far as I know, Mrs. Smith."

She hurriedly shut the door and slid the bar in place, turning at once and putting her back against it. Brandish thought he detected a sigh of relief, but if so, Ilsa Smith was quick to hide it. He went to the stove and opened his blouse to allow the warmth to flood in beneath it.

"Are you all right?" Ilsa inquired.

Brandish looked around the quiet room. Jamie was asleep on a blanket in the corner. Jane was probably likewise asleep back in the bedroom, where she would be near her brother if he needed her, for she had not appeared. "I'm fine."

"You've been away for hours. We were beginning to think you'd been. . . ." Ilsa didn't complete the sentence. What she had intended to say was plain enough.

"Is Miss Weston asleep?"

Ilsa nodded her head. "Finally. Poor girl's completely worn out."

Brandish pulled a chair back from the table. "She's not the only one," he said, and set the saber down and eased himself into the chair.

"What were you about out there?" she asked. Then her eyes discovered the blade of his saber. "Is that blood?"

He glanced over, seeing the dried brown streaks on the darkened blade. "I should have cleaned it off before I came in." His eyelids closed as if they had suddenly acquired a mind of their own.

"Apaches?"

He nodded wearily. "Mrs. Smith, would you be so kind as to wake me come dawn?"

"Yes, of course."

Brandish lowered his head to his folded arms and a moment later he was asleep.

Hair black as midnight, eyes wide and brown—curious eyes, like those of a wolf cub. Those wolf-cub eyes followed him as he strode across the parade ground, and suddenly Ethan Brandish came to a halt, as if compelled by an unseen hand to go no farther. He altered his course.

The Indian woman watched Brandish come near. She seemed to be burdened by a deep sadness, yet she remained tall and proud, standing there. Defiant, she was . . . and unmoving, like a statue carved out of an ancient tree. The hot wind stirred the hem of her cotton dress, and that was all. The baby in her arms with the wide wolf-cub eyes watched him coming across the empty parade ground too.

Brandish stopped, looked at her, and then at the baby bundled in the blanket in her arms. "Your baby?" he asked her. The voice sounded like someone else's, but the words were his own.

"My son," the Indian woman said.

Brandish caught sight of something buried in the blanket, and he moved aside a corner of it. Black shackles of iron encircled the child's wrists and his ankles. Brandish was stunned.

"Who did this?" he demanded.

The woman's proud eyes narrowed at him. They lifted then and her gaze traveled around the confines of the fort. Brandish did not recognize this place, but the lay of the buildings was somehow familiar. Her eyes came back to him and she said, "You have put the chains there."

All at once she thrust the baby into his arms. Fumbling, he got a grasp on the child. He was immensely heavy and cumbersome. The woman said, "Now you must care for him." She turned away and left him.

"Wait! Come back!" he called.

At his back, someone tapped him upon his shoulder.

"Huh?" He turned. His eyes widened and he nearly dropped the heavy burden in his arms. The once young, proud woman had grown old and sick, with gaunt cheeks and sunken eyes. Her fingers were like knobby twigs, and she was unsteady in the hellish wind. No longer proud, her spirit had been daunted, and ground down, like the stub of a cigar ground beneath the sole of a boot. Her withered mouth moved as if to speak, but no words came out.

"Where did you go?" he asked her.

"Away," she managed to say.

"How have you come to be like this?"

The sickened woman said, "I was taken from my land. Away from my gods."

"Who took you away?"

Again her eyes shifted and the pointing twig-finger circumscribed the parade grounds.

Still unfamiliar, this time something snagged a corner of his memory. His eyes stopped upon a house in the distance. A great house with white columns. And then he knew.

He looked back and the woman was gone, but at his feet the hot winds were scattering the small mound of dust that had not been there a moment before.

At his back someone tapped his shoulder.

"Huh?" He turned again. No one was there.

Again the tap. This time more urgent, it became a shove. Brandish wheeled, startled. "Who are you?" he demanded.

A vapor rose before his eyes.

"Captain Brandish?"

He shook his head. The fort melted away, and in its place stood Ilsa Smith, looking concerned.

"Captain Brandish," she said. "You asked me to wake you at dawn."

The vapor and the vision fled, and his brain cleared as he sat up. His muscles ached and he leaned back into the chair. "Oh, yes. But I just fell asleep."

"You've been asleep for hours," Ilsa said. "And it weren't no restful sleep neither. I declare, what was all that talking and carrying on about . . . a baby?"

"I . . . I must have been dreaming," he said, unable to shake the disquieting feeling that the specter had left with him. The back window shutters were open, and Ben Smith's Winchester leaned against the wall there. When he looked back at Ilsa, she seemed to read the question in his brain.

"Well, I couldn't very well let them Indians sneak on back and steal my horses, now could I?"

"No, ma'am."

"Captain?" Jane Weston had appeared in the doorway. "You're awake finally. Please, can you come here?"

He stood and reached for the saber, but it was gone. Ilsa had returned it to its scabbard and hung it on a peg by the door along with his hat and holster belt.

"I didn't want to leave it out where the boy could fool with it," she said.

"I suppose not."

"I cleaned it up for you, too," she added, sounding put out about it.

"Thank you."

Ilsa Smith wheeled about and folded her arms, staring at the sleeping child wrapped up in a blanket in the corner. Although she tried to control it, a shiver of fear ran down her back.

"You might want to continue keeping an eye on the corrals," he said. Doing something, anything, even watching three horses swatting flies with their tails, was better than standing around thinking about the next few hours.

Ilsa gave a low, bitter grunt and said softly, "I stopped doing what the cavalry told me to do years ago."

Chapter Sixteen

"The cavalry?" Jonathan Weston said weakly, his lips stretched back with the pain. The words sounded like a frog's croak, the voice like fingernails grating across a child's slate cipher board. His eyes were sallow and sunken and stared out from puffy, red sockets. They shifted, searching, found Brandish standing there, and then made their way back to Jane. "I don't understand, Janey."

"This is Captain Brandish."

The wounded man glanced again at the captain, and then slowly around the room, as if seeing it for the first time. "Where am I?"

"You're still at the Cohen Stage Stop," Brandish said.

Jonathan's hand slid up the covers and stopped at the place where the arrow had been removed.

His fingers explored the area, and appeared for a moment to once again touch the shaft. "Your men, they've secured the station, Captain?"

Brandish glanced at Jane.

"I haven't told him yet."

"What have you not told me?" Jonathan asked, suddenly anxious. He winced, shut his eyes tight against the pain, and nearly passed out again.

"There's no one else with me," Brandish said. "I arrived alone, two days ago."

Jonathan swallowed hard and parted his inflamed eyelids again. "Two days?" He glanced at his sister. "How long . . . ?"

"You've been unconscious three days."

He looked back to Brandish. "You removed the arrow?"

Brandish nodded. "Your sister helped."

Jonathan looked back at his sister, concerned. He said, "Are you all right, Janey?"

Brandish discerned the hidden meaning in Jonathan's words. He was convinced it had to do with her fear . . . with whatever it was that had happened to her in what he figured was the not so distant past.

Jane nodded her head. "I'm just fine."

Something unspoken passed between them and then Jonathan Weston brought his attention back to Brandish. "What's our situation, Captain?" He spoke with sudden vigor despite his weakened condition. A family trait, no doubt. Brandish had noted it in Jane that first evening, when he had come upon her and Jonathan in the barn and she had learned that he was by himself.

"With you conscious and on the mend, our situation has improved considerably."

"You're being evasive, Captain," Jonathan said, his voice gaining strength. "You don't have to be, not for my sake."

Brandish crossed his arms and leaned back against the bureau. "No, I suppose not. All right, I'll give it to you straight. We're in a devil of a mess. There are two dozen Apaches itching to get their fingers on your sister's scalp because she killed their leader, a renegade named Yellow Shirt. We do have a way out, but we can't use it because we'd never outrun the Apaches. And anyway, I dare not move you, Mr. Weston, at least not yet. In the next room is a woman and child. One just lost a husband, the other a father. We have food enough to last out a siege, but little water, and even less ammunition."

"And your men?"

"I have no men. Last week I retired from the cavalry. Like I said, I'm alone."

At his back, Brandish heard a sudden gasp. When he turned, Ilsa Smith was standing in the doorway, fingers grasping the jamb, her mouth a tight line, her eyes suddenly wide.

"I didn't know," she said.

"I didn't figure it made all that much difference, ma'am."

"But it does." Ilsa Smith's eyes fixed upon his a moment before glancing away. Brandish looked back at Jonathan. "So, you see, the outlook is pretty bleak."

"But not impossible."

Brandish grinned. He liked this man. Jonathan Weston was not a quitter. "No, not impossible."

He was aware of a flurry of movement behind him. Ilsa had hurried away.

"What are we to do, then?" Jonathan asked.

Jane grasped the wounded man's hand and squeezed it tight. The anxious look upon her face reflected her brother's concern. Now that he was awake, the resemblance between them was striking, and Brandish was amazed that he had not recognized them as brother and sister right off.

He unfolded his arms and stood away from the bureau, suddenly looking every inch a cavalry officer in charge of the battle to come, in charge of seeing that these people survived the fight. "For right now, our only option is to hole up here and weather the attack when it comes. That will give you time to gain some strength. At Fort Bowie, there's a sergeant who's going to start butting heads with a fresh-faced captain if I don't show up soon, and if that captain doesn't take out a patrol to find out why.

"But we can't stay very long," Brandish continued, tempering his encouraging words with a dose of reality. "It may come down to having to make a break for the fort. If it does, I'll have to figure out a way to give us some sort of edge. In any event, I want to give you at least one more day to build some strength before I stretch you

Brandish

out in the back of a heavily sprung freight wagon and hightail it to Fort Bowie."

"I'll be all right, Captain Brandish, I assure you."

Brandish grinned. "Considering the severity of the wound that you just survived, I don't doubt that for a moment."

In the next room a rifle suddenly barked.

Brandish dove out the doorway with Jane at his heels. At the window, Ilsa Smith was working the lever of the Winchester and sighting along its barrel. She squeezed the trigger and it fired again, leaping up against her shoulder, filling the room with acrid, gray smoke.

As Brandish grabbed up his Springfield, Ilsa said, "They were trying to steal the horses!"

"Did you hit them?" He sidled up alongside the window and looked out. The Apaches had already taken cover.

"I don't think so," Ilsa said, chambering another round. She was keeping well back from the window now. Someone had instructed her on how to deal with just this sort of situation. Someone who apparently knew a great deal about fighting Indians. Jamie crawled along the wall toward his mother.

Brandish said, "Take your post, Jamie."

He looked at his mother. She gave him a brief nod and he reversed directions.

"And keep your head out of that doorway," Brandish called after the boy as he scurried into the bedroom.

"What do you want me to do?"

Brandish looked over at Jane. "Cover the front window, just like you did yesterday. Keep in mind that that sawed-off scattergun has no range, but up close it cuts a wide swath. Don't go trying for any shots out beyond twenty yards."

He returned his attention to the corrals out back. Ilsa Smith looked grim and purposeful behind the long Winchester. The shutters opened across the room and Jane settled in place with the shotgun at ready. Brandish kept his view directed out back.

"The horses won't be easy to defend, if those Apaches are determined to have them," Ilsa noted.

"No, ma'am."

A rifle shot from a hidden location on the hillside gouged a chunk of wood from the shutter. Brandish and Ilsa flattened against the wall.

"Did you see where that came from?" Brandish asked.

"No."

Something moved on the hillside beyond the corrals. Brandish settled his sights upon a clump of sage brush there and waited.

Another shot drove him back from the window, and when he looked again, a single Apache had left his cover and was darting for the barns. The heavy Springfield roared in the close quarters of the stage station, and a hundred yards out the Indian jolted suddenly backward and dropped to the ground.

Brandish broke open the Springfield's breech

Brandish

and fed a fresh cartridge into the carbine's chamber. He measured the range to where the Apaches were moving about. The cavalry wasn't issued the heavier .45–.70 cartridges that the infantry used—for quite practical reasons. The cavalry carried the lighter, shorter carbines, and they kicked like a mule with the heavier cartridge—but at the moment he figured he could use the extra range that the heavier powder load offered, and to hell with the bruised shoulder that resulted.

"Keep your head down, Mrs. Smith," he advised, moving to the front window, where Jane Weston was crouched. He eased alongside her. She didn't shrink from him as he half expected. Clearly, attacking Apaches took precedence over cavalry captains. She had her head down below the sill, staring wide-eyed at the floor.

"Do you see anything?"

"No," she said.

"It's advisable to keep your head down, Miss Weston. But keeping it too far down is an invitation to the Apache to walk right up and lift your scalp." He snapped his finger. "Just like that."

She gave him a glare, and Brandish grinned. "Very good, Miss Weston. Now, direct that anger at the enemy. They won't give you much warning when they do come. Don't let them get too close." He left her there, retrieved his holster belt and saber from the peg by the door, and buckled them about his waist, adding a sixth cartridge to the revolver where he normally carried five, easing the hammer down gently on the live round.

The morning lengthened. A few desultory shots came into the building to remind them that the Apaches were still out and moving around. The sun climbed across the sky, scorched the land, and turned the station into an oven, but Brandish dared not open the shutters more than a crack.

He relieved Jane Weston at the window after a while so that she could tend to her brother. Jamie poked his head from the bedroom.

"Can I come out?"

The kid had been cooped up there all morning, and at least by the window, with the shutters partly opened, a small breeze made its way into the stuffy room. Brandish waved him over, told him to keep down below the sill. Jamie moved up against the wall and looked at him.

"I ain't heard no shootin'."

"They're playing cat and mouse with us, Jamie. They know we aren't going anywhere, and they're not ready to make a full frontal attack, not with us waiting for them to do just that. They're going to make us worry about it a while, firing just often enough to let us know they haven't gone away."

"Why don't they just attack? I thought that was the way Indians fought."

"Some do. The Plains Indians would—the Arapahos, Sioux, Cheyennes. They're fine horsemen, and they would have made skirmishing runs on this place long ago. But these are Apaches. If they have cover to fight from, and an enemy that's trapped, like we are, they'll use it to their advantage. You won't find a fiercer warrior than the Apache, and you won't find them presenting a large target to shoot at either, not when stealth will accomplish the same end."

"My papa told me about fighting Injuns in Kansas. He said that when he left the cavalry, he didn't want no part of fighting the hostiles no more. Said he wanted to live in peace and raise horses instead. But he taught me an' Mamma what to do just in case. I can shoot a rifle right straight, Captain Brandish, if you give me a chance—"

"Jamie!"

The boy looked over at his mother. Ilsa Smith had put her back against the adobe wall, the rifle across her knees where she could grab it up in an instant. She licked a bead of sweat from her upper lip and combed the long hair from her eyes, where it had worked itself loose from the bun atop her head. "You get the notion out of your head that you are gonna take any part in this here mess, understand, boy?" Her fingers expertly poked the errant strands of hair back in place and fixed them with the long, sharp pins driven through the knot like spears. As she spoke, she kept her attention directed out the window, at the precious horses that for the moment were content to finish up the hay Brandish had tossed out to them the evening before.

"Yes, ma'am," Jamie said, disappointed.

When Jane returned to the window some time later, Brandish gave her the post again, and he went across to Ilsa.

"Why don't you walk out the kinks a while, Mrs. Smith?" he said, settling near the window.

She looked surprised by the offer, and seemed unsure what to say. She nodded her head and moved away from the window.

Chapter Seventeen

Ilsa Smith took a drink from the small keg of water in the corner. She put the dipper back on its hook and dried the perspiration from her face with a well-used handkerchief that she carefully refolded and returned to a pocket hidden beneath the pleats of her wrinkled skirt. She brushed at a spot on the skirt and frowned at the fruitlessness of trying to make the garment into anything other than what it was—old and worn.

Ilsa walked about the small room to work the stiffness from her legs, feeling suddenly old and worn herself. She tried not to think of Ben, or the loss his death had brought to her and Jamie, but a hole had opened up in their lives. What was she to do now that he was gone—what was Jamie to do?

Every time her gaze came across Brandish, the

blue uniform that he wore, the silver bars on his epaulets, her anger flared.

Ben had wanted what Brandish had more than anything—the esteem that rank brought. He had been a good soldier. Loyal and absolutely brilliant when it came to understanding the enemy. But because he had been a man of color, the rank of sergeant was the most he could ever hope to attain.

And Ben and Ilsa had wanted more out of life for themselves—for Jamie. Especially after all those lost years beneath the oppressive hand of a white master before the war had finally broken the shackles that had kept them bound to that plantation in Georgia—bound and bent to the will of another man! But even in the cavalry, a free man, Ben had been bound by shackles—not of iron, but of color.

He had been a better leader and soldier than those who had commanded him. Ilsa bristled remembering how he had reached as far as he could ever go in only a few short years. Not that promotions ever came quickly in the United States Cavalry. Ilsa had been a soldier's wife and she understood that. But at least for the white man, perseverance and ability could eventually lead somewhere.

For the black man, the top came quickly, and it wasn't very high. Ben had been proud to serve. The Ninth Horse Cavalry had fought brilliantly. Just the same, they had been called *nigger troops*. Ilsa had heard it with her own ears from the mouths of the very men who had fought to set her people free! Even now, rage swelled within her at the recollection. How quickly they had thrown the black man back in chains. Fancy words on a piece of paper was all the emancipation amounted to.

She struggled to pull her thoughts back to the moment, and to her son in the next room. She must protect Jamie at all costs. Just the same, every time she saw Brandish, the words *nigger troops* rang in her mind.

Ilsa discovered that her pacing back and forth had brought her near Jane's post. She stopped, standing beside the window, where she was out of the line of fire, and peered down at the white woman. To regiment her thoughts and take them off brooding over the past, Ilsa asked, "How's your brother faring?"

"He's still awake . . . and very worried."

Ilsa laughed briefly. "Well, at least we know that that Apache arrow didn't affect his brains. It seems a sensible thing to be worried now."

Jane smiled weakly, but didn't say anything.

Ilsa noted the underlying sadness in the young woman's face. She recalled the odd anxiety that seemed to grip Jane like a palsy whenever Brandish happened to come near her. Ilsa lowered her voice and said, "You want to talk about it?"

Jane glanced up, startled. "Talk about what?" She feigned surprise, but her lowered voice matched Ilsa's own conspiratorial tone.

Ilsa inclined her head across the room where Brandish had stationed himself near the back window. "Him. What ever did he do to you, child?"

"Captain Brandish? Why, he hasn't done anything to me."

"Perhaps not him then," Ilsa said, certain now that she was on the right track, "but some man obviously did something to you . . . and not all that long ago either, if I'm any judge."

Jane's face blanched and she glanced away. "I'm sure I don't know what you are talking about, Mrs. Smith."

Ilsa Smith lowered herself to the floor. "If you don't want to talk about it, that's all right by me. But sometimes it helps." Ilsa wondered if it was Jane she was trying to help, or herself. It seemed that by some peculiar twist of fate, they both had been highly disturbed by the same man; a man neither of them had met until only a few days before.

Ilsa cast a glance in the cavalry captain's direction. He was a tall man—taller than most that she had known who wore the uniform of the United States Cavalry . . . except for her Ben. Brandish's brown hair was showing streaks of gray, but his age did not appear in the face, or in the gut, where it begins on most men. He looked grim at the moment, staring out that bright slash of light formed by the half-opened shutters—and with good reason. His mouth was a hard line beneath a salt-and-pepper mustache, his eyes deep and hooded beneath a scowl.

And like her Ben, Captain Ethan Brandish had quit the cavalry.

Why?

Brandish had attained the rank of captain!

Brandish

What her Ben wouldn't have given to be able to wear proudly those epaulets with the two silver bars of a captain in the United States Cavalry.

Ilsa stood and said, "I guess I'll take a look in on Mr. Weston, and see how Jamie's faring." If this white woman didn't want to unburden herself, Ilsa Smith certainly wasn't going to force her.

Lord knows, I've been takin' on other folks' misfortunes long enough. Time someone comes to lend a hand with mine.

Ilsa could see clearly beyond her own immediate grief. She would have hard times now that Ben was dead. There would be no one for her to turn to. Ruby and Frank had been friends who didn't notice color, but they were dead. Ruby, Frank, Ben . . . everyone. Any family that Ilsa might have known had either been killed during the war, or sold off before.

"Mrs. Smith?" Jane said.

Ilsa paused at the doorway and looked back. Brandish glanced over from the window, and immediately returned his attention to the hot, dusty grounds beyond.

Jane touched the hard earth floor and Ilsa lowered near to her. "There is something," Jane said, barely above a whisper, and her large blue eyes shifted to make certain that Brandish hadn't heard her.

"Tell me, child."

Jane looked back out the window, but Ilsa Smith knew she wasn't seeing the endless stretch of sage and mesquite, or the hot sand, or the wavering air that lay out there where the Apaches, like the coyotes, lived and thrived. Hardship, Ilsa had come to learn, was as necessary as food and water to the Apache—as it seemed to be to the black man. Perhaps that was why she and Ben had gotten along so well out here.

After a moment, Jane Weston spoke.

"It was four months ago." She began slowly, almost choking on the words. "Jonathan and I were living with my father on a small piece of land near the Canadian River. It was a pretty spot, because we had water in what's mostly dry land and stiff grass. Good cattle country, but not so hospitable for a dry-land farmer. And father wasn't much of a farmer, but he did understand stock, much like your Ben did, I suspect. We didn't have enough land to run cattle, so he turned to horses." She laughed briefly, looking into Ilsa's dark eyes. "I guess when you think about it, we two are very much alike."

Ilsa wanted to tell her they were not at all alike. Jane was white and Ilsa wasn't, and that placed a world of difference between them. But she held her tongue.

Jane averted her eyes out the window, as if the view beyond the shaded porch and crippled stagecoach made what she had to say easier. "Jonathan had taken the buckboard into town for supplies. I had intended to go with him, but Father suddenly came down with one of his frequent attacks of gout, so I stayed behind to be near him if he needed help. . . ."

Brandish

"Go on," Ilsa prompted when Jane fell into a long silence.

She blinked away from the harsh sunlight outside, and her hand lighted upon the barrel of the shotgun in her lap and slowly wrapped about it, tightening, as if something within her was trying to strangle the weapon.

"We didn't often get visitors way out where we lived, so when they came, I was wary, but Father welcomed them in. To water their horses was all they wanted—or so they claimed, but right off two or three of them set out around back of the house where we couldn't see them. All together, there were eight—and I'll never forget their faces. Rough strangers who had been on the move a long time. Their clothes and manners showed it. Their horses needed rest.

"The leader was a—" Her words suddenly caught in her throat. "—a man named Darius. Darius Chipwell. He was friendly right off, but something about him set the hairs lifting off my neck. Father offered them the water, directed them to the dirt tank behind the corrals. It was kept full from a culvert he'd built from a flowing artesian well up the hillside."

Jane suddenly started shivering. She struggled to bring her body under control again. "The ones that had gone around back must have been checking to see if there was anyone else around, but we were alone. Father had a rifle set just inside the doorway. He always kept it there just in case, but these men seemed interested only in watering their horses and being on their way.

"All at once the ones that went around back came through the house and out the front door to where we were standing on the porch. Father got a glimpse of them a moment before I did, and he turned on them and raised the cane that he used whenever the gout returned—" Her voice faltered, and a bit of moisture came to her eyes. She wiped it away with her sleeve.

"The one that came through the house first never hesitated. Not for a heartbeat. He shot Father. I . . . I remember it so clearly. Even now, like a dream that moves horribly slow, I see him flung backward by the bullet, see the back of his vest ripped outward, and the bloody, ragged hole suddenly there—and to this day, I do not know why these men did what they did."

Ilsa put a hand lightly upon Jane's shoulder. The younger woman swallowed heavily and seemed to gain strength. "Afterward, they took me. They dragged me into the house, threw me onto Father's bed." She stopped again, remembering, and rubbed her wrists as if to free them of something.

"What followed isn't very clear in my memory, but at night I sometimes dream, and wake up screaming. They used the leather laces from Father's boots. They tied them so tight I swear I thought they would surely cut off my blood, and that my feet and hands would die. That first day I know I wished for death a thousand times over." Again, Jane's words seemed to catch in her throat. She struggled and squared her shoulders and said, "They each had their way with me, and then some more, and when they got bored of that, one of them went out and found a rake handle and—" She could go no further.

Ilsa took the sobbing woman into her arms, and as she held her close, she was aware of Brandish at the window watching the two of them. What did he think? The hell with what he thought. Ilsa comforted Jane, and curiously, she suddenly resented her earlier thought. Perhaps she and Jane were very much alike.

Jane got control and dried her eyes. "They finally left after I don't know how long. Days, it seemed. Jonathan found me there, still tied to the bedposts. He took me into town, to the doctor, and for a while they didn't know if I was going to live or die. I bled for weeks afterward. But after a while I grew strong again." She gave Ilsa a weak smile. "I should say my body grew strong. I . . . the woman inside me . . . that woman is still back there at the house. I fear she'll always be back at that house."

Ilsa said, "It gets better, child. I know."

"You do?"

Ilsa nodded.

Jane smiled feebly. "I pray that's so."

She took a long breath that seemed to calm her. "Jonathan and a number of men from town tried to follow their trail, but they never did find them. Afterward, after I recovered, I refused to return to the house, except once, to put flowers on Father's grave. Jonathan wanted to stay, I know, but for my well-being he suggested that we move away, far away. So, here we are, on our way to California. They say California is the golden state, where a person can make themselves into whatever they want to be—only, it's not, really, is it?" She looked out the window again at the bleak Arizona desert stretching away in all directions.

Ilsa frowned and didn't know how else to help this tortured woman. In the end, she used Brandish's own advice. "Keep a sharp eye now, child. We'll make it out of here, and you'll be on your way to California."

Jane tried to smile, but there was no vitality in it.

Ilsa stood to return to her station.

From somewhere outside, a shot rang out.

Ilsa reeled backward and around. The ceiling and floor swirled together into a single blurred image, and she fell to the table and brought it crashing down beneath her.

Chapter Eighteen

Jane screamed, dropped the shotgun, and clasped a hand over her mouth.

Brandish wheeled and the next instant, an Apache sprang through the open window where Jane had gone rigid. He had a knife in his hand, and was lunging for the woman as she sat there, suddenly immobile and terrified.

Brandish swung the Springfield toward the Apache, and it roared like a mountain howitzer going off inside the station. The Indian lurched backward, out the window, and sprawled across the porch out front.

Jane had crumpled to the floor, paralyzed with fear, her eyes wide and staring at Ilsa Smith.

Ethan Brandish was at Jane's side. "Snap out of it!" he yelled, taking her by the arm. He dragged her from the window and slammed the shutters, driving home the bolt.

Through the back window, a second Apache was thrusting the barrel of an old cap-lock trade rifle at them. Brandish dove aside, pulling Jane with him as a spray of adobe mud erupted from the wall and stung his cheek. He leaped across the room, swung his rifle as a club, caught the Indian in the head, and knocked him unconscious to the floor. Immediately a third Apache was diving through the opening.

Brandish drew his revolver and again the small room reverberated, and gun smoke thickened in the hot air.

He heard them at the door, saw the heavy wood strain beneath their efforts. The ex-captain flung open the breech of his rifle and shoved a fresh cartridge into the chamber. In a glance, he appraised the situation. Two Apaches lay inside the station, dead, or near it. Huddled in a corner, Jane Weston's wide eyes told him she would be useless now. Ilsa Smith was under the rubble of the table, unconscious. Dead or alive, he did not know. Somewhere behind him, he heard a small voice calling.

"Mamma?"

"Stay back in the bedroom, Jamie!" Brandish barked, leaping to the open window.

A swift figure in leggings, with an eagle feather fluttering in his long braid, dashed across the clearing between the station and the barns. Another moved down near the corrals. Brandish drew a bead on the first man and dropped him.

The second Apache was near the horses. If they succeeded in stealing the animals, there would be no hope of escape. He broke open the rifle, but the extractor ripped away the rim of the spent cartridge, leaving it jammed inside the chamber.

Brandish cursed the weapon and tossed it aside. Poor extraction—or poor ammunition—was one of the venerable Springfield's major shortcomings, and it had caused more than one battlefield casualty that he knew of. He grabbed up his revolver and fired out the window. The Apaches in the corral dove for cover, but the range was too great for anything that approached accurate shooting with a revolver.

Brandish cursed again and glanced at the heavy, barred door. He could hear them pounding on the other side, but it would take more than a few strong shoulders to bring it down. He grabbed up Jane from the corner of the room where she huddled upon the floor, crying uncontrollably.

"Snap out of it!" he yelled, partly because the gunfire still rang in his ears. He thrust the shotgun into her hands and set her near the back window. "Don't let anyone come through here! Do you understand?"

She did not seem aware that he had spoken to her.

Brandish shook her. "Answer me! Do you understand?" Jane blinked up at him, staring blankly, and brought her sobbing under control. "I said don't let anyone through this back window."

She marshaled her strength, got control of her emotions, and nodded her head. Finally she managed to drag her wide, staring eyes from Ilsa Smith.

"The window. Forget everything else. They must not come through that window."

Jane Weston was drawing on whatever little reserves of fortitude she had left. "I understand, Captain," she said, looking back at him.

"Good." The tension in his voice eased some. Brandish turned to the back window and looked into the yard beyond. He fired his revolver at a sprinting figure, and another Apache stumbled and fell. Others now were moving toward the horses.

"It'll be up to you to keep this station secure, Miss Weston," he said, replacing the spent shells in his revolver. He hoped the restraint in his voice would help her muster her own resolve.

"Me?"

"I have to secure the animals." He had no time to explain further, and bent through the window, straightening up outside, his back against the adobe of the stage station.

A bullet sang past his head. He flinched, spun around, and his revolver bucked in his fist and brought down the Indian coming around the corner.

Brandish dashed into the open with bullets spraying dirt at his feet. An arrow thudded some-

Brandish

where nearby. He dove behind an oak rain barrel and fired back toward the stage station where a face had appeared. The Apache there retreated around the corner. Coming about, he fired again, heard a howl, and saw the Indian grab his thigh and hobble back out of sight.

Brandish made a leap for the corral. Two Apaches were busily herding the animals toward a section of fencing that a third man was hastening to disassemble. The ex-officer's bullet put him down, temporarily securing the corral. The two remaining warriors abandoned the horses and turned savagely on him, drawn knives glinting in the lowering sun.

Brandish swung his revolver to them and pulled the trigger again. The hammer snapped harmlessly on a spent cartridge and the expressions on the Apaches' faces changed at once. His revolver was empty, and now, weaponless, he would be an easy kill for them. They came boldly forward.

Brandish was aware of another Apache crawling through the rails to his back. He holstered the empty revolver and stood erect before his challengers. Suddenly, as if the participants of the battle were struck with curiosity as to the outcome of this confrontation, the gunfire ceased, and the three Apaches closed in, bent, stalking him like a pride of mountain lions might a cornered deer.

Brandish drew his long saber, and its bright curved blade reflected the red of the lowering sunlight as if it had already tasted blood.

There ist, in mortal combat only, a true avakening of von's senses. You must allow yourself clear thought. The veapon vill move as if alive, but only if you allow it to do so. Nicht, *not so tight. Do not strangle it. Hold it lightly, like it ist little bird. Gently! Like you hold the young* Mädchen *vhen you vhirl them across the dance floor.*

It was odd that he should recall von Kliner's instructions so clearly now, as if the old Prussian was standing at his side, whispering to him.

One of the Apaches dove forward. Brandish came around with a slashing parry. Their steel blades rang together and the Apache somersaulted away, instantly back upon his feet with the swiftness of a cat.

The veapon knows where it must strike next.

Brandish wheeled and lunged. The Apache that had sprung for his back came to an immediate stop, his eyes stretched wide with surprise before he died. Brandish wrenched the saber free again, dripping red with its third baptism of blood. The first Indian made a second try, and suddenly it was as if Brandish was back on the fencing strip with von Kliner—both instructor and opponent—teaching him the secrets of the art of saber combat.

He lowered, and as if it were an old dance step, perhaps a bit rusty, but never forgotten, he lunged, kicking forward. The whole motion seemed to amaze the Apache, who drew up for an instant to discern what this crazy white soldier was up to. But it was an instant too long, and before he was able to leap aside, Brandish's blade had pierced his chest and his heart, and he died still on his feet.

Brandish turned to confront the final Indian, who had crouched warily and was circling now, knife moving side to side like a snake about to strike.

From the stage station, the twin boom of the shotgun came like thunder. Brandish kept his attention riveted upon this last opponent, and he was only distantly aware of a figure on horseback rushing down the hillside at them. But he dared not take his eyes from this deadly adversary.

Some unspoken warning rang in his brain, and Brandish dove aside a moment ahead of the arrow that buried itself in the dirt where he had been standing.

The rider veered away and at the same time the Apache crouched before him screeched and rushed forward, his blade held low to drive upward.

The saber flashed, slashing downward, moving without conscious thought.

The veapon knows vhere to strike.

The saber stopped with a violent shudder. Brandish felt it clash against hard bone, heard the grisly cry. The Apache's fingers sprang apart.

The knife fell from his grasp and his other hand clutched the half-severed wrist.

The Apache looked at the point of the saber, red now with the blood of his brothers, then he looked up at Brandish. Grimacing from pain, the Apache stoically erased all signs of his anguish from his face, and scowled defiantly into the ex-soldier's eyes.

He showed no fear of death. He was a warrior, and ready to die like one. It would have been a simple task now for Brandish to take his life. A swift lunge was all that was required.

The two men considered each other. Back at the stage station the shotgun boomed again. Perhaps no more than a second or two actually passed before Brandish knew that he was not going to kill this man. There was no need to. Instantly, Brandish swung the flat of the blade around. It slapped the Indian across the forehead and knocked him unconscious to the ground.

Brandish made a sweeping about-face, his saber ready, but no more warriors had come to challenge him. Then he spied Rock That Sparks off in the distance, sitting astride his pony, watching the battle—watching Brandish.

He had no time to think about that. The next moment an arrow sang past. Brandish plunged through the corral rails and made a running dive into the open side door of the barn. Instantly regaining his feet, he pressed up against the wall of one of the stalls, sheathed his saber, and pumped six bullets into his revolver, snapping closed the loading gate and thumbing back the hammer.

Brandish

Back at the stage station, the shotgun fired once more, followed by the sharper report of the Winchester . . . once . . . twice came its higher, sharper voice. Brandish knew he had to make it back to the house now. He had visions of Apaches clambering through the open window faster than Jane could feed fresh shells into the shotgun. As a last-ditch effort, he figured she had turned to the rifle.

From somewhere outside the barn came the pounding of hooves. Something made a bright arc through the glassless window and landed in the hay pile in the corner.

Brandish leaned out the window and fired. The rider dropped, but immediately another Apache was coming. This puzzled the ex-officer. It was not the Apaches' preferred way of fighting.

Behind him, the hay pile had burst into flames. From outside another torch whirled into the barn, and then a third. Brandish scrambled out the window of the smoke-filled stall.

Another torch cartwheeled through the air and landed in the back of Ilsa's buckboard, atop a canvas tarpaulin folded there. Brandish dodged toward it, but an arrow streaked past and buried itself into the side of the wagon, driving him to the ground. Coming back to his feet, another feathered shaft whistled overhead. He had only a moment to return fire, which cleared a path for him back to the house, and although he hesitated half a second, regretting the loss of the buckboard, there was nothing he could do about it now. Already flames were feeding on the dry wood.

Brandish jogged across the yard beneath a tempest of gunfire. With no regard for what he might find on the other side, he flung himself headlong through the open window and crashed to the floor beyond, landing like a circus acrobat, and in a single roll was again up on his knees.

He came face-to-face with the gaping bores of the double-barrel shotgun, and Jane's narrow blue eyes squinting at him over the barrels.

"Get your fool white head down, Mr. Brandish!"

Ethan was momentarily confused, for Jane had not spoken a word, but he prudently obeyed the order. The shotgun bellowed, and the Apache that had appeared at the window immediately disappeared.

Brandish glanced around, and to his great relief and pleasure, he discovered Ilsa Smith glaring at him. She had propped herself up with her back against the wall, and that long Winchester rifle was in her hands.

"Darn fool, Officer. You nearly got your head blown off!"

Chapter Nineteen

Brandish didn't tell Ilsa Smith how pleased he was that she was still alive, for immediately a howl that set his blood surging brought his attention back to the window. The rifle in Ilsa's hands fired almost at once, adding its portion of smoke to the already acrid air, and the Apache tumbled back.

Jane shifted her position and the mighty roar of the shotgun bellowed out the front window. Brandish took the rifle from Ilsa's weak fingers, working the lever as he moved up alongside the window. Two Apaches dropped beneath his careful aim. He was conscious of the need to conserve ammunition.

The battle had taken a turn, and the Apaches were retreating. He tried to calculate how many of the Indians had been put down, but exact numbers were impossible to determine.

The two barns were aflame, and along the hillside out back, Indians were dashing for cover. Brandish picked his shots with care, and when the Winchester's magazine was empty, he handed it over to Jane and took up the shotgun, but the Indians had moved out of range now. They seemed to be regrouping. Then he spied Rock That Sparks upon his pony, beyond rifle range, holding a war lance overhead.

Brandish took a long breath and lowered the hammers on the shotgun. "They're sounding recall," he said. He suddenly remembered Ilsa Smith.

She had slumped back to the floor, lying in a pool of blood growing beneath her. Brandish said to Jane, "Give me a hand here."

"Now what is it you're tryin' to do to me?" Ilsa protested weakly as he and Jane eased her prone onto the floor.

"Please don't struggle, Mrs. Smith," Jane said, placing a comforting hand upon the woman's moist brow.

"Where are you hit?" Brandish asked.

"My leg is burning like sin, Captain Brandish," Ilsa said, and then she glanced at him sharply. "Now you keep your hands off me. Miss Weston can look."

"This is not the time to concern yourself with modesty," Brandish said, pulling at the volume of material that constituted Ilsa's dress, and the petticoats beneath it.

"Captain Brandish is right, Mrs. Smith," Jane

said soothingly. "I'll be right here with you."

He felt the weight in the clothing now as he lifted away the blood-soaked material. Ilsa winced and gritted her teeth, and Jane took her hand and held it with reassuring firmness.

Brandish found the wound eight inches above her knee. He ripped away a strip of cloth from the dress to use as a tourniquet. The bullet had made a clean hole through Ilsa's leg, and although there was much blood, Brandish saw immediately that the wound was not life-threatening.

He said to Jane, "Get the whiskey."

She hurried into the back bedroom, and when she came back, Jamie was with her, all wide-eyed and on the verge of tears.

Brandish said, "Your mother will be all right, Jamie."

The boy was staring at the blood. Blood always made a wound look worse than it was. Brandish had learned early on to look past the blood when treating battlefield casualties to determine the true seriousness of a wound.

"It's a flesh wound. No broken bones, and it doesn't appear any arteries were cut," he said, cleaning away the blood. He could see the hole clearly now that the tourniquet had stemmed the bleeding.

Jamie knelt beside his mother and took her hand. Ilsa smiled at her son through the pain, and told him he was a brave boy.

"This is going to hurt," Brandish said. But the sting of the alcohol would be nothing compared to the pain Ilsa was enduring already.

Ilsa managed a short laugh. "It can't hurt more than having a baby, Mr. Brandish."

"I wouldn't know about that, ma'am," he said and spilled the whiskey into the wound.

Ilsa flinched and stiffened, and tightened her grip until Jamie whimpered. Afterward, breathless, she said, "Well, maybe just a little more."

"Keep pressure on the tourniquet," he told Jane, and took the Winchester back to the window. When he moved, he was aware of a sharp pain on the back of his arm, as if a dozen bees had all lighted on the same place at once, and when he looked, he heard Jane exclaim, "You're wounded too."

Brandish rolled up his sleeve. There was a furrow in his skin where an Apache bullet had grazed him.

"Jamie, hold this for me," Jane said, and the next moment she was pushing him into a chair by the shattered table and shoving his sleeve farther up. "Here, let me see it, now. My land, you're acting like a child."

"I'm okay."

"Captain Brandish, you yourself said wounds need to be treated, especially to stop infection." She grabbed up the whiskey bottle.

Brandish eyed the little bit left sloshing around the bottom. All at once he was not so convinced anymore.

"Now, give me that arm," she demanded.

He complied grudgingly, and when she poured the whiskey into his wound and he let out a little yelp in protest, he was certain he heard a muffled laugh escape Ilsa Smith. Jane fixed a proper bandage around his arm before she released him.

"I think it hurts worse after the cure than before," he said.

"Men!" Jane huffed.

Brandish put the pain out of mind and spent a long moment peering out the window. Night was almost upon them. The barns were being consumed in a roaring conflagration; flames leaped through the windows and crawled along the roof timbers. Soon there would be nothing left but the burnt adobe walls, but the fire would keep the grounds bright for several more hours.

The horses had retreated to the far end of the corral. They were out of danger from the flames, but nonetheless on the verge of panic. Brandish doubted the nervous animals would allow the Indians near them anytime soon. Still, if the Apaches did manage to break down the corrals, there would be no keeping them from bolting.

It was an impossible situation. So far, he had been able to keep the animals secure, and themselves alive, but he could not hope for his luck to hold out very much longer. They might be able to defend this position one more day, but after that, they would run out of ammunition. And waiting for help to arrive was a fool's game.

Frowning, Brandish turned away from the window and took a tally of where they stood: Two wounded, a terrified boy, a woman battling some private war within herself, and one retired cavalry officer.

The wagon out back was now a pile of charred timbers. He counted up their remaining ammunition and discovered what he had already feared. They were perilously low on everything but the .45-.55 cartridges for the Springfield.

He retrieved the carbine from the floor and worked the stuck cartridge from its chamber with the point of his barlow knife. Then he ran a brush and a patch through the bore to clean the powder fouling, which most often was the cause of cartridges sticking in the Springfield chamber, and reloaded it.

Unbarring the front shutters, Brandish surveyed the yard in the lengthening shadows. The Apaches had departed. He went out onto the porch.

The clay olla that hung from the beams overhead had amazingly survived another battle. Brandish dipped out a drink of water and considered the overturned stagecoach in the yard. All the spars and the riggings he had devised were still in place. The Apaches apparently saw no reason to dismantle the affair, knowing as well as he that the coach was a hopeless means of escape.

He checked the loads in his revolver, shoved it into his holster, and with a wary eye for any lingering Indians, returned to the station to drag the two unconscious Apaches outside and over by the blacksmith's hut.

Daylight finally gave way to the night.

Brandish strode out to give the wrecked coach another look. It didn't take but a minute before he had made up his mind as to what had to be done next.

"How are you feeling, Mrs. Smith?" Brandish asked when he returned to the stage station. Ilsa looked comfortable enough sitting on the floor, her back propped against the wall. Jane had fetched a pillow for Ilsa's head and had taken up the shotgun again, dividing her attention between Mrs. Smith on the floor, and the yard out back.

"I hurt real bad, Mr. Brandish, but I've hurt worse and made out all right."

He grinned. "You've got spunk."

"Got to, I reckon, to survive out here," she answered.

"Think you could move if you had to?"

"With a shoulder to lean on?"

"I think we could manage one of those."

She looked at him curiously. "What have you got in mind?"

"Getting out of here."

"Now?"

"Tonight."

Jane looked over. "But what about Jonathan?"

"We're going to have to risk moving him."

Despite her concern, Jane Weston appeared to understand the need. "Ilsa's wagon has burned to the ground," Jane pointed out.

"We still have the stagecoach, and three horses to pull it with. If we don't make a break for it tonight, tomorrow may be too late. I can't protect the horses and us in here much longer."

"The sun has most surely gotten to your brain,"

Ilsa said. "Ain't no way you're gonna get that stagecoach up onto its wheels, even with all that fancy buildin' you did out there. And even if you could," she reminded him, "how do you expect to outrun the Apaches?"

That was the question.

The time had come for Brandish to take the battle to the enemy's front door and eliminate that one remaining problem. "I've got an idea about that," he said, "but I'm going to need your help—all of you, and that includes you too, Jamie. But first we need to move you somewhere safe, Mrs. Smith. I'd guess there is room enough in that bed for two, wouldn't you, Miss Weston?"

"Now what's that you say?" Ilsa gasped.

Jane said, "I'll give you a hand."

Ilsa fiercely protested. "I'm safe and comfortable right here on the floor, thank you. Mr. Brandish. I'll not share a bed with a strange man."

"He is that at times," Jane agreed.

Brandish nodded his head. "Well, if that's the way you want it, but you may not think it's so safe and comfortable if you get stepped on."

"Stepped on?" She eyed him. "Who's gonna step on me, Mr. Brandish? You?"

Brandish grinned. "No, not me. But the horses just might."

Chapter Twenty

Ilsa agreed that a move was probably advisable, and after some haggling over the matter, she compromised on a chair by the stove where she insisted that she was adequately comfortable. Brandish took that to mean that sitting in a chair was superior to being trampled on by nervous horses, and it was certainly preferable to sharing a bed with Jonathan Weston.

After she had been moved and her leg carefully propped up, Brandish clasped Jamie on the shoulders and hunkered down to eye level with the boy. "Your ma is okay for the time being, Jamie. Think you can give me a hand gathering in those horses?"

"I'm right good at handling stock, Captain Brandish," Jamie said.

"Now hold up there a minute," Ilsa intervened

from her throne, leaning forward. "You're not takin' *my* boy out there in the dark with hostile Apaches about!"

"They've regrouped, Mrs. Smith. For a while I believe we have some room to breathe. I know the Apaches, ma'am, and my guess is they won't try for us again tonight. They will, however, try for the horses—after those barns burn down and the grounds darken. They know that if they were to try for them now they'd be easy targets, and the Apaches are too cunning for that."

Ilsa plainly did not like the idea, but the excitement in her son's eyes was something even a worried mother could not ignore. And helping Brandish was something to take his mind off of his grief as well, if only for a while. "Ben always did say I coddled the boy. Reckon I don't want to raise no sissy," she said, relenting. "But mind you, Mr. Brandish, if one hair on that darling head gets hurt, I'm holding you responsible."

Jamie Smith needed to feel useful now. After all, he was about to take up the role of man of the house. And the ex–cavalry officer knew that Jamie's mother understood this too. Ilsa Smith was a wise woman, and he would have told her so—but she'd only deny it and tell him to mind his own business if he had. Brandish kept the sentiment in reserve. Sooner or later she'd overcome whatever it was about him that bothered her. "I'll take care of Jamie, Mrs. Smith."

Ilsa huffed and cast her view over at the window where Jane had traded the shotgun for the

Brandish

Winchester and the greater range it offered. Jane had showed no interest in using the Springfield, and Brandish credited that to the woman's good sense, and the value she placed on her shoulder over the weapon's superior stopping power.

"How does it look out there, Miss Weston?" Ilsa asked.

Jane glanced over. "All quiet so far. The smoke and flames have made the horses jittery, but they haven't spooked."

Brandish found the remains of the bedsheet they had ripped into bandages for Jonathan and tore off three wide strips. He shoved them in the waistband of his trousers. Then he and Jamie went outside to the stagecoach and gathered up a coil of rope left over from his engineering project. They carried the gear around back.

Brandish took note of the rifle barrel poking through the back window, but he felt little reassured by it. If he had misjudged the Apaches this time, would Jane see the approaching danger and be able to dispatch it before it got too close to them?

"Captain Brandish?"

He glanced at the small boy hurrying to keep up with him. "Yes, Jamie?"

"How long have you been fightin' wild Indians?"

"How long?" Brandish grinned. "I reckon since the war ended. I just went from fighting one kind of enemy to fighting another."

"Why are the Indians our enemy? Why do they want to kill us?"

Brandish paused in the darkened yard with the red light of the burning barns leaping across his face, and Jamie's. He thought a moment, then said, "I don't think the Indians want to kill any more than you or I. It's just that now they have their backs up against a wall with nowhere left to go. In the early days, there were always those whites—" he paused, then added, "—and Negroes who had their bouts with Indians. But the incidences were rare compared to the times when Indians and settlers would meet and trade and travel in peace.

"For the most part, when civilization moved too close for their comfort, the Indians would pack up and move farther away. That very thing happened out here with the Apaches for a long time. It wasn't really until after the Bascom affair that we began to have serious troubles with the Apaches. Before that, leaders like Cochise and Mangas Coloradas managed to get along with the flow of settlers."

They resumed toward the corrals.

"But then, why are Indians so bent on killin', Captain Brandish?"

"Bent on killing? Where did you hear that from?" He had a feeling he was about to hear another one of those truisms—like Jane Weston's theory that the Apaches never attacked at night. But Jamie just shrugged his shoulders and looked up at Brandish with his big, brown eyes.

"I don't know where I heard it."

They had come to the corral. Brandish stopped with his boot on the bottom rail and said, "In battle, Indians kill other Indians and whites and blacks alike, just like every soldier in every corner of this world does, but they have a curious custom that I've never heard of among any other soldiers or warriors. Do you know what that is?"

Jamie shook his head. "No, sir."

"Well, it is called counting coup—actually, I don't know what the Indian word for it is, the early French explorers gave it that name—and what it amounts to is hitting or touching an enemy in battle. Not killing that enemy, mind you, but just touching him, with a stick, or if they are very brave, with their hand, and then escaping alive afterward. Why, they figure that there's more honor in that than in killing off a dozen men. Now you tell me, Jamie, doesn't that sound like a very civilized way to fight a war?"

"I ain't never heard of that before, Captain Brandish."

"Well, it's true."

"Then they aren't always killing?"

"No more than I'm always killing, or your pa was always killing when he was soldiering with the Ninth."

Jamie winced, and Brandish could tell he was remembering. The ex–cavalry officer nodded his head at the horses beyond the rails, and pulled the boy's thoughts away from his loss. "Well, Jamie, let's get these critters rounded up and over to the station where we can keep a better eye on them."

Cooing softly, he and Jamie eased into the corral. Jamie showed understanding beyond his years in the careful way he approached the nervous animals. Ben Smith had taught his son well. They got a rope around one of the animals. Brandish snubbed him down to a post and tied a strip of sheet around his eyes. This settled the nervous animal, and Jamie fashioned a halter out of the rope they had brought along while Brandish went on to the next horse.

In ten minutes they had all three horses ready for travel and brought them without incident around front, and with some urging, up the steps and into the station. All at once the small size of the room became apparent. Brandish pushed and shouldered until he had them against the wall away from the stove, and with considerable effort ran the ropes up over a viga, which was about the only item in the station sturdy enough to tie the animals on.

"What would Ruby say?" Ilsa scolded, shaking her head in disapproval over allowing horses in the house. Jane thought it amusing, though only her smile revealed this to Brandish. He put Jamie in charge of them and unbuckled his saber and placed it against the wall.

"You're going out again, aren't you?" Jane asked, the brief glint of amusement suddenly fleeing from her eyes.

"I have to if we're going to have any chance of making it out of here."

"Couldn't we just board up tight and wait for help?"

"It could be days in coming, Miss Weston, and we don't have days."

"We have provisions, and we can store water."

"Perhaps, but our ammunition is low, and how long do you think it will take before the Apaches finally knock the door in, or hack a hole in the roof?"

"He's right," Ilsa said from her chair.

Jane frowned and glanced back out the window. The fires had about burned themselves out, leaving a pile of embers that had once been the wooden roofs of the two barns, and would glow softly for days. "I know," she said reluctantly.

Brandish thought a moment then took up the saber and put it in Jamie's hand. "You better keep this handy, Jamie."

The boy's eyes brightened as he turned the sheathed weapon over.

"If the Apaches do come back, your ma and Miss Weston are going to need all the help they can get."

"Yes, sir!" he said.

"Captain Brandish," Jonathan Weston called from the other room. His voice sounded stronger.

Brandish stepped through the doorway and looked down at the man in the bed. "I almost forgot you were among the conscious again, what with all the excitement." Brandish grinned, put a scuffed boot on the bed rail, and leaned over. "You have good color."

Jonathan gave a short laugh and said, "How can you tell in this light?"

Brandish moved the lamp closer, studied him a moment, nodded his head, and set the lamp back. "Yep, you have good color. I say you look much improved."

"But not nearly enough for what you're planning, isn't that what you're thinking? I may be a prisoner of this bed, Captain Brandish, but I'm not deaf . . . or blind."

"That's not at all what I'm thinking. What I'm thinking is that it's a miracle you survived this long. I'd say you passed over the danger yesterday and look well on your way to mending. I've seen many a man with less of a wound die. I've seen maybe one or two with worse live. There's no calling it. Like the toss of dice, there's no way of knowing what the numbers will be. You were lucky, or maybe the Almighty has future plans for you, or maybe you just have the resilience of an old army mule. I don't know, but I don't think being jostled about for a few hours in that stagecoach out front will do you in now."

Jonathan frowned. "That's encouraging." His voice lowered and his view shifted past Brandish and toward the doorway. "How's Janey bearing up?"

"She's bearing up well—as well as can be expected, all things considered."

Jonathan's attention returned to Brandish. "She's had a bad couple months. I don't think all of this could have come at a worse time."

"I know."

"She told you?" Jonathan Weston sounded surprised.

Brandish shook his head. "No. Not in so many

words. But it's plain that something's happened to her."

"Yes. Of course. It would be. Jane would never mention it to you, and perhaps I shouldn't either. Only . . ." He paused as if sorting through his thoughts. "Only, if I should not happen to make it—well, Janey is fragile right at the moment. She's really a very strong person, Captain Brandish, and she'll be strong again, I'm certain. It's just that now she needs time to heal, and to know she's safe. I vowed to protect her at all costs. But now it looks as though I might not be able to keep that pledge."

"Are you are asking me to watch over her if you don't make it?"

"No," he said at once. "I would never impose like that. I just wanted you to understand the situation, and perhaps you could see that she was taken somewhere safe. We have an aunt in California. She has a letter from me that explains everything, and she knows we're coming." He considered his next words carefully before continuing. "I know the cavalry has many rough men in it, but you seem to be a gentleman. Believe me, Captain Brandish, Janey cannot bear the attentions of men. Not now, at least."

Brandish said, "You know, I have yet to hear you say a word of concern for yourself."

Jonathan made a wry smile. "She's my sister." The way he said it explained it all.

"Well, don't go despairing yet, Mr. Weston. With your luck, I wouldn't be at all surprised if you we are the only one who makes it out of here alive." He grinned. "I'd like to have you nearby the next poker game I sit in on. I promise you, Mr. Weston. If anything happens to you, and I'm able to, I'll see that she gets safely on her way to California."

Jonathan laughed softly. "If I was all that lucky, I wouldn't have gotten myself shot in the first place, now would I? Thank you, Captain Brandish."

Brandish turned to leave, but drew up in the doorway and swung around. "In the meantime, Mr. Weston, you try to get some sleep. When we do leave here, you're going to be in for a rough ride."

"Don't worry about me, Captain."

"No, I suppose I shouldn't."

Brandish emerged into the main room and wrinkled his nose. Ruby would be turning in her grave if she knew what he had done to her once meticulously maintained house, but it couldn't be helped. Bringing the animals into the small station was a last resort—or was it the last act of a desperate man? Brandish wasn't sure anymore.

Jamie, still holding the sheathed saber, looked up at him, and for some reason the boy appeared just a little older. In the chair, Ilsa bit back her pain and showed him a stern face. She had acquired the shotgun in his absence, had it in her lap, with the remaining few shells in the porcelain washbasin on the floor at her side.

"What are we to do while you're away, Mr. Brandish?" she asked.

"Keep the place shut tight is all. When I get

Brandish

back, we won't have much time. You and Miss Weston will have to be ready to leave at once. Miss Weston, Jamie, and I will use one of your horses to right the coach. Once on our way, all of you will ride inside. That stagecoach won't stop a bullet, but it ought to keep arrows out."

"You really think that contraption you built out there is gonna get that buggy back on its wheels?"

"I sincerely hope so, Mrs. Smith . . . for all our sakes, I sincerely hope so."

Brandish tugged on his hat and left.

Chapter Twenty-one

Not only was the moonlight shining brightly off the smooth-surfaced pond, but Brandish now had to contend with the soft red glow of the ember pile out back that only a few hours earlier had been a pair of sturdy barns. Only their adobe walls remained, black and ragged now with their roofs collapsed inside them.

He lingered in the shadows of the stage station until his ears and eyes grew accustomed to the night. Although he was fairly certain the Apaches had withdrawn to lick their wounds, there could be a couple hidden in the darkness, waiting, watching. He had to risk that. They had only one hope of escaping the Apaches, and Brandish knew what he had to do.

Brandish jogged away from the house and dropped to the ground behind the ranks of ocotillo that stood beyond the yard. He waited, his senses alert, and when he was certain he hadn't been seen, he moved away slowly, making a wide circle around the red, flickering heap out back, all the while keeping his revolver in hand, ready at an instant's notice.

He gained the foot of the hills without incident, and upon reaching the heights he stopped to study the way he had come. The stage station below was nearly invisible against the blackness of the night, except for the faint threads of light that escaped the barred shutters. The glowing remnants of the barns stood out starkly, appearing at a distance like the arrested flow of lava from some recent volcano.

Ethan Brandish moved away, dodging from shadow to shadow, keeping to the edge of the ravine where the moonlight could not reach him. In what seemed no time at all to him, he had worked his way, on his belly, up to the rim of the valley where the Apaches had set up camp.

In the long hollow below, fires burned, and men moved about in earnest enterprise. The last time he had observed them from this very spot it had been a quiet camp. Most of the Apaches had been asleep then. Now there was activity with a purpose. Braves were repairing arrows and war lances, women were treating the wounded, and above the low chanting voices coming from a group sitting around one of the campfires, Brandish could hear muffled talk, and the occasional groan from one of the half dozen casualties of the battle. Among the wounded, he recognized the Apache he had fought in the corral, and had allowed to live. His wrist was wrapped with a poultice, and another bandage had been fixed about his forehead. He would not be joining the battle anytime soon, and after taking careful count, Brandish identified only fourteen warriors still able to carry forward the attack.

He located Rock That Sparks speaking with a small group of warriors, his generals, Brandish assumed, and there were probably more than a few recently brevetted among them, considering the heavy casualties they had suffered. The Indian leader had a Spencer repeating carbine across his knees, a prize rarely encountered among these southern tribes, where most weapons were of the outdated caplock trade rifle variety.

The ex–cavalry officer's attention moved from the Indians to the horses that had been gathered in the brush corral at the head of the valley. The animals were guarded by two men. Brandish studied the layout long and carefully until he was certain there were only those two guards. Moving as quietly as the smoke that rose from their campfires, Brandish made his way to a position above the corrals and settled in to wait.

The horses seemed unaware of him, or if they had picked up his scent, dismissed it as no threat. He had been long enough away from soap and water to not cause them alarm. He had begun to smell like the Apaches, and the smoke from the torched barns that clung to his clothes only helped his scent blend with those about the campfires.

Making no sound, he drew his knife and eased toward the nearest guard. He positioned himself, gauged the distance, and lunged. In a swift movement, he muffled the Apache's mouth and drove the knife into his heart. The man struggled a short moment in Brandish's powerful grip, then went limp. Brandish withdrew the knife, feeling warm blood on his hand, and quietly lowered the dead Indian to the ground and wiped off his hand and the knife handle.

Other than the soft nicker of a nearby horse, the brief scuffle had not betrayed him. But he had little time left now. The presence of the first guard would soon be missed. Brandish advanced on the second man, and in the space of a heartbeat, this Apache too lay dead among the stiff, dry grass.

The animals backed nervously away when he slipped through the brush corral and hurriedly removed the branches that served as a gate. Seeing the way open to them, the horses circled toward it. Brandish caught the mane of the last horse, swung up on its back, and in the same instant unholstered his revolver and fired into the air.

The sharp report of his revolver electrified the camp, and a moment later the pounding of approaching hooves spurred the Apaches into motion. Men and women leaped aside, grabbing up the wounded and their weapons as the herd swept through camp with Brandish in the rear, one hand twisted in the flying mane, the other holding his Colt revolver. He swung toward an Apache nocking an arrow into his bow and fired again. The arrow careened off and the Indian went down.

The animals drove on through the camp, breaking apart fires, sending spark-showers flying into the dark sky. Brandish and the horses passed through the camp, ahead of the reports of rifles, but soon that sound died down and he heeled the horse beneath him, shouting and driving the mounts out of the valley and onto the open plains. After a mile, he swung away from the fleeing herd and rode hard for the stage station.

Brandish leaped off the sweating back of the winded animal and sent it on its way with a sharp slap to the rump. He bounded to the porch and knocked on the door. "It's me," he said, not waiting for the question to be asked of him from the other side, and when it opened, he pushed on past Jane and immediately began untying the horses.

"Any problems here?" he asked as he worked.

"No," Jane said.

He brought one of the animals around and stopped, looking at the two women and the boy. "I bought us a few hours at best, but we need to be out of here at once. Some of them will be making their way on foot." He glanced at Ilsa. "How are you doing?"

"I'll make out."

Brandish

"And Jonathan?" he asked Jane.

"He's ready."

"Good. Now, help me with that coach."

Jane, Jamie, and Brandish took one of the draft horses out front. He had rigged up a harness to the main line that ran up to the block and tackle. In a minute, with Jamie's expert hand with the horse, they had it strapped into the harness.

Brandish guided the horse forward and took up the slack, then he put the horse in Jamie's hands. The boy urged him on. The animal strained. Jamie clucked softly to it.

"Keep up a firm, even pull," Brandish told him. The boy knew how to make the horse respond. The rope tightened, the spars bowed.

Brandish caught his breath as the old wood creaked. Then the stagecoach moved. It groaned and seemed somehow dismembered, as if someone had taken a scalpel to the huge bug. It lifted on its leather suspension. The spars arched over and something snapped, resounding like a firecracker.

The horse strained. The coach came up, and for a moment the huge wheel bowed, taking the full weight on its edge.

The horse stopped and took a step backward.

"Keep the rope taut!" Brandish shouted, and leaped behind the half-uprighted coach, putting a shoulder into it, his legs straining.

The horse dug in again.

"Keep him moving!"

Jane was suddenly at his side. She seemed

small in the darkness, with her hands clutching the spokes of a wheel nearly as tall as she was. But there was determination in her eyes and in the set of her mouth, and lines of strain cut deep into her face.

The horse kept up a steady pull that a breed of any lesser size could not have long endured. Slowly Brandish felt the stagecoach rising on its side. He heard the spars creak again, and groan overhead. If one should snap now, both he and Jane would be instantly crushed beneath the two-thousand-pound Celerity coach. He put that thought out of mind and strained at the lifting coach.

Leather and wood sang out and with a sudden rush and thump, the coach rocked over and dropped heavily onto its wheels. Brandish heard a heavy sigh. When he looked over, Jane Weston was grinning at him.

"We did it!" she cried.

The sheer excitement in Jane's face had turned it from plain to beautiful. He lifted an eyebrow at her. "You sound surprised." Then he grinned and drew his sheath knife and freed the coach of the ropes attached to the spars overhead. He went around to help Jamie strip off the halter from the horse.

"Bring the others out," he told the boy and Jane. He tied the horse to the front wheel and began sorting through the tangled traces. He had them laid out when Jane and Jamie brought the other two animals over. Brandish harnessed Ilsa's matched horses together, and put his

Brandish

lighter cavalry mount in the traces ahead of them. There'd be some difficulty controlling the coach with the team unmatched, but that couldn't be helped.

As he buckled the horses in place, Jane came from the station with an arm about Ilsa Smith. She helped Ilsa up into the open door and passed the rifle and shotgun in after her, and finally Jamie, with two canteens slung over his shoulder and Brandish's saber in hand, crawled up with his mother.

Jonathan was another problem. The man endured the trip out to the coach without a word of complaint, but the pain had been almost more than he was able to endure, and when Brandish and Jane had him laid out on the floor, with a pillow beneath his head, he let slip a muffled groan and passed out. Brandish put a hand on the bandages on his chest, but they had remained dry. That was a good sign.

Jane started into the coach, but Brandish said, "I want you on top with me."

She glanced up at the high narrow seat and appeared to go rigid. "Shouldn't I remain with Jonathan, inside? Earlier you said we all should ride inside."

"I changed my mind. Mrs. Smith can keep an eye on him. When the Apaches catch up to us, I may need an extra hand."

"When?"

"I don't think there's any doubt that they will. Fort Bowie is still a long ride, and there's not much in the way of civilization between here and there. You know how to drive one of these?"

She shook her head. "No, of course not. But if it's anything at all like a buggy—"

"It's not." He grabbed her arm, felt it turn to ice beneath his grip, and helped her up into the seat. He slammed the door shut, and Ilsa's black face and big eyes stared out at him from the forward window.

"It'll be a rough ride," he said.

"You do what you have to," she said. "I'll do my best with Mr. Weston."

Jamie's face appeared in the other window. "I'll protect 'em, Captain Brandish," and he showed the hilt of the saber through the opening.

Brandish grinned at him. "You know what a brevet is, Jamie?"

The boy shook his head and looked blank.

"It's a field promotion in rank given during a time of war, or a battle. Of course, they don't give you any more money to go along with it, just a new title. The military doesn't give them out anymore—not officially, that is—but I suppose in your case we can make an exception."

"But I've got *no* rank, sir."

"Well, you do now, Lieutenant Smith."

"Lieutenant?" Awe was in the boy's voice, and his eyes went wide.

"Now, Lieutenant Smith, you take care of your ma, and Mr. Weston, you hear?"

"Yes, sir!"

Brandish

As he left, Brandish noted the scowl on Ilsa's face, but she kept her disapproval to herself. He figured that, at least, was a step in the right direction.

Chapter Twenty-two

The coming of dawn faded the black vault overhead to blue-gray, and one by one the stars winked out until only the bright fire of Venus was left to be extinguished against the spreading smudge of pink already tingeing the horizon to the east. Ethan Brandish drove the horses on at a steady pace, but with restraint. The coach was monstrously heavy, designed to be pulled by six mules. These three horses were doing double duty, and if he pushed them the way he wanted to—the way he knew he had to, they'd tire out long before reaching Fort Bowie.

On the seat beside him, Jane Weston had spoken little since leaving the stage station. Brandish understood the private thoughts a person reviews at a time like this.

Brandish

He had managed to give them a head start. If luck was with them, the Apaches would only now be rounding up their scattered horses. They'd still be hours behind. But Brandish wasn't going to count on that. He peered over the tattered canvas top of the rocking stagecoach, at the old Butterfield Road that stretched behind them, but the darkness of the night just past still clung to the land, and he could see nothing in that direction.

But Brandish had no misgivings. They would come.

During the hours that had passed since leaving the stage station, Brandish had handed over the reins to Jane Weston twice. She'd learned the feel of them, the pull of the horses, and she knew what she had to do to keep the stagecoach running straight in spite of the lack of a second animal paired with his own. The experience had been good for her in more ways than one. It had distracted her from thoughts of the Apaches . . . and from whatever had happened in her past that tortured her so.

Now he handed the reins over again. She came out of her trance and took them automatically. Lines of concentration came to her face, and the cords of muscle in her arms tightened as she assumed control.

"Not bad," he commented.

"It isn't so different from a buggy after all," she noted, "once you get the feel of it." Jane glanced over and smiled.

He reached down to the floor of the front boot

and came up with his carbine. The smile faltered and Jane returned her attention to the indistinct road ahead.

"You still expect them?" she said.

"I do."

"It's been hours."

"They'll be here. I only bought us a little extra time. Not freedom."

"Perhaps we would have been better off staying where we were."

He looked over his shoulder, but the darkness back there still revealed nothing. "Maybe. When it's all over we may have wished we stayed. Hindsight is like that, pretty clear and perfect. But there comes a time when you have to make a decision and the devil take the consequences."

"A decision that involves other people's lives?"

He glanced over at the quizzical look upon her face, not certain what she was getting at.

Jane went on quickly, "That is what you've been trained to do, Captain Brandish, is it not?"

"It is, indeed, Miss Weston."

She studied him a moment before turning back to the road, growing more distinct with the waning night. Brandish considered her words. Making decisions with other people's lives is what he had been doing half his life, and he wondered if that wasn't one of the reasons he had decided to retire from the military. He could find no answer within himself, and he returned his vigilance to the wide, open land slowly emerging from the shadows around them.

Brandish

* * *

It was ten to ten by his watch, and the sun was already hot in the morning sky. The horses drew them along, growing weary beneath the relentless pace and the burden of a swaying ton of timber and canvas on wheels, but they were splendid animals, and they strove on under his gentle urging. Just the same, their progress had slowed. Brandish had considered more than once pulling up and giving them a rest. Then he would think of Rock That Sparks, and his warriors, and settle instead for letting up some on their pace rather than giving them the rest and grazing they truly required.

Brandish shut the lid to his watch and shoved it back into his pocket. Suddenly the report of a rifle cracked off to the right of the stagecoach. He'd had no indication they were so near, and considering the open landscape, he found that amazing. His head came around and he saw the mounted Apaches to the right of them, angling in toward the coach, riding hard.

Another rifle boomed. Brandish wheeled about to see a second contingent of warriors coming in fast on his left flank.

Brandish snapped the whip and the coach lurched ahead, but the three tired animals were no match for the swiftly approaching Indians. He handed the reins over to Jane, grabbed the iron hand hold, and fighting the swaying pitch of the coach, switched places with Jane so that she'd have access to the brake lever.

Brandish pushed his carbine over the top of

the flapping canvas roof and drew a bead. The heavy rifle boomed and punched him in the shoulder.

He ejected the hot shell, fed in a fresh round, and fired again. Sporadic rifle fire came in, but their bullets went wide. The Apaches suffered from the same problem as he; they couldn't aim well off the backs of their pounding horses. Brandish had one advantage though; he could reload his weapon rapidly. Only Rock That Sparks had a repeater, and the sharper report of his Spencer was distinctive.

Brandish flinched as a sound like an angry bee buzzed past his ear.

From below he heard the chatter of Ilsa's Winchester. An Apache flipped backward off his pony. Brandish concentrated on his shots. His Springfield boomed again and another Apache careened off his horse.

He continued a steady barrage, not hitting much from the rocking coach, but keeping them back. The Springfield's barrel was growing hot. After another couple of shots from down below, Ilsa's rifle fell suddenly silent, and the Apaches swarmed in again.

Brandish braced his Springfield across one of the iron bars of the luggage rack. An arrow sang in and impaled the seat near his leg. His next two shots dropped as many Apaches and the Indians drew back out of range of his powerful carbine.

Brandish glanced at his ammunition box and frowned. There was only a handful of rounds left.

Brandish

He'd have to conserve what little he had left. But to what end? To prolong the inevitable? Death at the fearsome hands of the Apaches was never swift. He swept aside that thought, snapped open the trapdoor of his carbine, and fed another round into the smoking chamber.

The coach lumbered on, but the horses seemed to have lost the rhythm of their stride. Ilsa's repeater remained silent below, and only Brandish's continued fire kept the remaining Apaches at bay.

"The team's slowing. I can't make them go any faster!" Jane shouted at him above the rumble of the wheels, her voice on the precipice of panic.

He kept his attention on the targets wavering past his sights. The Apaches drove in again, seeing their advantage in the failing animals. Brandish kept up the volley until his ammunition ran out.

The Apaches numbered less than ten now, and they seized the advantage. An arrow thumped into the coach, and another was deflected by the ironwork around the top of the coach. Brandish took over the reins and urged the horses on, but they had no more to give. Rock That Sparks and his warriors swept recklessly near, and an Indian not a dozen feet off to the left of the coach drew his bow.

From below came the thunderous twin boom of the shotgun. The Indian lurched off the back of his horse.

So, Ilsa still had some fight left in her after all.

Then the sharp, high-pitched voice of the Spencer rifle spoke somewhere nearby. Brandish came about in time to see Rock That Sparks rein his horse aside. In another moment, one of Ilsa's big horses stumbled. A streak of crimson glistened down his flank. The horse caught himself, stumbled again, and went down beneath the coach.

The seat lurched beneath him, and the next instant Brandish was tumbling through the air. The sound of splintering wood and crying horses seemed to be chasing him. When he hit the ground, he managed to do so on his feet, and with only enough time to scramble away before the stagecoach crashed to a sliding stop and was instantly engulfed in a billowing cloud of dust.

In the confusion, he saw that Jane had landed apparently uninjured. She was shaking her head as if stunned, only slowly getting her bearings and crawling on hands and knees toward the twisted coach. Its great rear wheel was spinning freely in the air, and through the flashing spokes Brandish saw the Apaches approaching.

He dove for cover behind the coach as an arrow whistled nearby. An Apache charged past, war lance thrusting out. At that moment, Jamie's head poked out of the upturned window, and the next instant the lad was clambering out of the coach, Brandish's long saber still in his hand. Brandish reached for it and in one swift move drew it from the steel scabbard and swung about, severing the war lance as it drove past.

Jamie dropped to the ground, and Ilsa's panicked voice called for the boy from somewhere inside. The Indians were suddenly swarming around the coach. Brandish fired his revolver and his blade flashed and drove like the shuttle of an automatic weaving machine.

His revolver clicked on a spent shell. His saber hit bone and momentarily lodged there. He had hardly the strength to withdraw the blade. A movement caught his eye, and he wheeled about to face an Apache coming over the side of the coach.

With black eyes, long, wild hair, lips drawn and a howl of Satan, the Apache stood tall on the side of the coach, aimed his war lance, and cocked back his arm. Brandish had faced death many times, but never like this. Never had he been both disarmed and helpless to do anything about it.

At the same instant the Indian launched his weapon, the sound of thunder boomed behind Brandish. The Apache's motion was abruptly arrested and violently reversed, and the war lance clattered to the ground at Brandish's feet. The Apache disappeared behind the coach and Brandish wheeled about in time to see Jane Weston breaking open the action of his Springfield, precisely as he had instructed her earlier, and feeding in a fresh shell from the small cache in her pocket. The Springfield fired again, knocking her half around. Another Apache plowed into the ground, and at the sound of the big gun suddenly back in service, the remaining Indians withdrew and regrouped beyond its range.

Chapter Twenty-three

"Jamie!" Ilsa Smith cried when her son did not at once appear.

Brandish had helped her from the shattered stagecoach and sat her down against the exposed undercarriage and thoroughbraces.

"Jamie! Where's my boy?" She looked about the wreckage with panic-stricken eyes.

Brandish had not noticed that the boy was missing. Startled to discover him suddenly gone, he glanced around too. He had seen Jamie emerge from the coach during the heat of the battle, but he had immediately lost sight of him when the Apaches had swarmed in.

"Where's my son?" Ilsa was shouting, grabbing at the thoroughbrace, trying to pull herself to her feet. Jane withdrew her head from the open stagecoach door where she had been tending Jonathan, and she and Brandish made an immediate search of the grounds around the coach.

The boy was not there.

Brandish found the saber's scabbard that Jamie had been clutching lying some distance away.

Ilsa managed to gain her feet. Brandish pulled her back, for she was trying to hobble out into the desert. "They've taken Jamie," she was crying. "They've taken my boy!"

"You can't go out there!"

"I have to!"

"Please, Mrs. Smith, get down," Jane said, and Brandish perceived that in spite of her own fears, she was trying to be a voice of reason in this impossible situation.

"We'll get him back," Brandish said.

"They'll kill my son!"

For all Brandish knew, Jamie may have already been killed. He swept that notion from his brain. There was no understanding the Apache mind in time of battle.

A whistling sound, now frighteningly familiar, reached Brandish's ear. He dragged Ilsa Smith back behind the coach a moment before the arrow arched overhead and buried its point in the hard ground a few feet away. Brandish grabbed up his Springfield and fired, but the Apache was already racing away from the coach, lying low along the off side of his horse.

Brandish put out a hand, and as if able to read his thoughts, Jane dropped the remaining three rounds of carbine ammunition into it. He reloaded the carbine and his revolver. Between the two weapons, he had a mere eight shots left. He had recovered the shotgun from the wreckage, but there were no more shells left for it.

The Apaches kept up the skirmishing passes all morning. In the intervals between the volley of arrows and occasional bullets, Brandish and Jane managed to lift Jonathan Weston from the coach. He seemed barely alive. His wound had begun to bleed again, and he did not regain consciousness when Jane spoke to him.

They laid him in the shade of the coach, but that was not about to last, as the sun moved relentlessly toward noon.

Their horses were dead. The wreck of the coach, and the Apaches' first attack had seen to that. Among the ruins, Brandish recovered the only one of the two canteens that had come through the ordeal intact, but its water would not last long in this heat.

Ilsa Smith was consumed with despair. She withdrew to someplace inside herself, whimpering softly as she hugged her knees. Jane tried to console the woman, but Ilsa only chanted Jamie's name softly between the tears, and occasionally Brandish heard Ben's name too, as if Ilsa was consulting with her dead husband.

Brandish had tried to bring them to safety, but he had failed. He cursed himself silently for having made the attempt. They were trapped here just as they had been back at the stage station, only now they were exposed, and it was only a matter of hours, no longer days, before they would be overpowered.

The Apaches knew this as well, and they also knew that given enough time, the sun would do for them what their arrows and bullets had not been able to accomplish. He squinted at the glaring fireball overhead. Soon it would turn this land into a foundry's furnace. His thoughts traveled back to those forts up north, and the coolness of the country there. He recalled his yearning then to move south where he did not have to contend with freezing winters and the frostbitten toes, noses, and fingers that regularly accompanied those extended patrols in the more northern climes. Right now, though, those past outposts seemed most attractive.

But the Apaches would not have to wait for their slow death by the sun. Brandish's ammunition was nearly spent. His shots had gone wide as the Apaches had kept up their careful and swift skirmishing attacks, and through it all, their strength had remained at seven.

They know what they're doing.

Rock That Sparks seemed to understand that they were down to a handful of shots, and afterward, when the ammunition was gone, he and his warriors would ride boldly in and easily conquer these invaders of his hostile land . . . his home.

Brandish grimaced. He was going to lose this last battle, but the Apaches were destined to lose the war. They could never resist the relentless squeeze of the United States Government and its people, hungry for more and more land, and the wealth hidden beneath it. Oddly, Ethan Brandish felt a sorrow for these men even now as they sat out there on their ponies waiting for the opportunity to kill him and the people he had hoped to protect. It was a regret that he could not explain. Over the years of fighting the Apaches, he had grown close to them, had begun to understand them in a small way that most whites never would. . . .

A shrill war whoop pierced the hot air. Two warriors pounded near on the backs of their ponies and released arrows that thumped into the coach. Brandish fired the last round from the Springfield, but they had moved out of range again. He set the carbine aside—perhaps in the end it would serve again as a club, but for now it was useless—and palmed his revolver. He had kept careful count of his shots, but just the same, he rechecked the loads in the cylinder.

The end was near. He saw that Ilsa had not come out of her trance. She had been a powerful aide to him despite her hostility, but now as the black woman's strength had drained from her, Jane Weston had grown stronger. Jonathan had said she was a strong person, and would be again. Brandish had recognized it in her that first evening when she realized it was up to her and him alone to save her brother. Jane Weston was a woman who could draw fortitude from adversity. A good woman to have at his side.

"They say it's an awful thing to die at the hands of the Apaches," Jane said softly.

He wished that he could reassure her that that was not true. He leaned back against the undercarriage of the stagecoach and looked at the revolver in his hand. Three bullets left. Jonathan was still unconscious. He'd never know what finally killed him. But he had to consider Ilsa and Jane. At the very least, he could save them from suffering any further.

As if knowing his thoughts, Jane said, "You would not be contemplating that if you were alone." There was reproach in her eyes.

Her perceptiveness startled him. "I'm not alone," he said, "and it's true what you just said. It's a terrible thing to die at the hands of the Apaches. What would you have me do?"

She started to speak, then stopped and shook her head. "I don't know. You're the officer, the leader, the one who is supposed to know that. What would you do if you were alone?" She fell silent, staring out at the wide, bleak land beyond.

What would he do if it was only himself to worry about?

Suddenly he knew.

The Apaches made another skirmishing run, firing their rifles, then veering away. Brandish took careful aim at the fleeing warriors and fired. His revolver boomed three times. When he retreated back behind the stagecoach he gave Jane a frown and set the revolver beside the Springfield—two bold symbols of the modern army—

but the Apaches, armed with only their primitive weapons, had won this time.

He saw the question in Jane's eyes, and she seemed to read his reply in his own face. It was only a matter of minutes now.

Another skirmishing attack came, and it went unanswered. That would tell Rock That Sparks what he wanted to know.

Then for a while there was silence.

Ilsa Smith came out of her grief momentarily and grabbed hold of the thoroughbrace and hauled herself up to peer over the side of the overturned coach. Immediately she gave a cry of alarm.

Brandish rose to his feet, knowing what to expect. Rock That Sparks and the tattered remains of his war party had reined to a stop not a dozen yards off. What did surprise Brandish, however, was the bundle one of the warriors carried under his arm.

Jamie Smith was still alive! Stricken with fear to be sure, and only the tears that streaked his face and glistened in the harsh sunlight showed that the boy was still breathing and healthy. Beyond that, terror had turned the boy rigid, and even when the Apache dropped him to the ground, Jamie Smith remained paralyzed with fear.

One of the warriors lowered the point of his war lance to the boy's chest and Rock That Sparks came a few steps forward and reined to a stop.

"Jamie!" Ilsa cried and tried to hobble out to

the boy. Brandish held her back, and she glared around at him.

"I'll talk to him," he said.

"Talk?" Ilsa's face registered shock. "Talking isn't gonna save my boy!"

"Please, Mrs. Smith," Jane said, gently pulling the woman back down.

"No. At least allow me to watch."

"We will both watch." Jane stood at Ilsa's side. Beyond the stagecoach, like figures carved from sun-weathered wood, the mounted Apaches remained motionless in the noonday heat.

Rock That Sparks considered the wrecked coach, and then the survivors. His gaze shifted to Brandish and he said, "Blue soldier. You fight brave."

"Rock That Sparks had many brave warriors. I regret that they had to die."

The war chief nodded his head.

Brandish said, "Does Rock That Sparks kill children?"

"Blue soldiers kill Apache children, and Apache women."

"This is not good," Brandish said. "The Great Father in Washington does not wish his blue soldiers to kill Apache women and children. He wishes the Apache to live in peace, on the reservation."

The war chief shook his head and his hair, decorated with bits of bone and feathers, slid heavily across his shoulders. "I will not go there. The reservation is death for my people. I will remain free."

Brandish

"Well, we each do what we have to."

"I do not want to kill you, blue soldier. Give me yellow-hair woman and I will allow you, Raven Woman, and her little one to live."

Brandish heard Jane gasp at his side. Her face paled suddenly. He put a hand upon her shoulder and said to the chief, "I will not give you this woman."

"Then the boy dies first. Afterward, you will all die."

"No." Brandish stepped out from behind the coach. A glint of sunlight upon the ground caught his eye. He bent and came up shaking the dust from his saber and placed himself between the coach and Rock That Sparks. "I will never give you the woman, but I will trade my life for the life of the boy and the woman. It will be that only, or you will have to kill me here where I stand to get to them. The choice is yours." Brandish drew himself up straight, standing tall and unflinching, the curved sliver of steel in his hand catching and reflecting the sunlight.

Rock That Sparks considered his words, his face stern, not revealing the direction of his thoughts. As if at once coming to a decision, he reined his horse about and rode back to his warriors.

Brandish had taken the long shot, counting on the Apache's respect for bravery, but his offer had been a sincere one, and now he would know the result of this last desperate act. The moments passed like long eons on a paleontologist's calender. Suddenly one of the braves cried "A-he!" thrust his war lance into the air, and dug his heels into his horse's flanks.

The animal leaped into a full gallop and instantly the warrior was bearing down on Brandish.

Chapter Twenty-four

He had struck the bargain, and he would stand by it. To fight now would have been useless. With only the saber, he might have taken one or two more with him, but then surely they would kill Jane and Ilsa, and Jamie and Jonathan too. Brandish readied himself for death.

The shrieking Apache drew nearer. He let out a long, chilling war whoop, and at the last minute shifted the war lance aside and soundly struck Brandish on the shoulder with a short stick. The warrior swept on past him, reined his horse about, and galloped back to the others.

A second Apache drove the point of his war lance into the ground and left it there as he let out a yelp and propelled his horse forward.

The animal came close enough for Brandish to feel the warmth of its sweating body, and again he was struck, and he reeled to one side from the blow. The warrior returned to his companions, retrieved his war lance, and thrust it to the sky.

It was at once clear to Brandish what they had in mind, as one by one they took a turn at him, striking him and letting out a yelp of triumph.

They were counting coup! When the last of the warriors had counted coup on him, Rock That Sparks urged his horse forward and drew rein at Brandish's side.

Brandish ached in half a dozen places, but he remained unflinching, looking the Apache war chief in the eye. He dared not show Rock That Sparks anything but a stoic face. He dared not destroy the impression of bravery, or the coups would count for nothing, and there would be only one recourse left to them.

For a long moment the two men considered each other, and finally the Indian reached out and counted his own coup on Brandish, not with a stick, but by hand.

Then Rock That Sparks looked down at him from the back of his horse and said, "Blue soldier. You are a brave warrior. From this day, your name among the People will be Long Knife, Killer of Many Apache. I give you the life of the yellow-hair woman. We will meet again in battle."

"I do not want to meet you in battle, Rock That Sparks, but in peace. I will look forward to the time we sit across from each other, smoking a pipe in friendship."

Brandish

The war chief slowly shook his head. "I will never live on Crook's reservation." The Apache leader heeled his horse about and rode off, and his warriors followed after him.

In a minute they were but specks in the distance, and then the wavering heat and stirring dust swallowed them completely, and Brandish was alone. He rubbed his aching arm, and the sore spots on his side and chest and shoulders, and went to the boy they had left behind. Dropping the saber, he helped Jamie to his feet. The boy was unharmed. Brandish brought him back to his mother, who instantly smothered him in her arms and drenched him with her tears.

"What was that all about?" Jane asked, still shaking from her fear, and more than a little confused now.

Brandish grimaced and said, "It's something called counting coup. Jamie knows all about it, don't you, Jamie?"

The boy managed a weak nod of his head, and that was all.

"Well, I don't. Tell me," Jane said.

"To the Apaches, and to other Indians as well, it is a far braver thing to touch a worthy warrior and live to tell about it, than it is to kill that enemy. You see, in their minds, now they will have another chance at me."

She seemed bewildered, but let it go and asked instead, "Are they going to come back?"

"No. As far as they're concerned, this little war is over, and they were the victors."

"But that doesn't make sense."

"It does to them, and that's all that matters."

Brandish frowned and said, "How's Jonathan?"

"He's still unconscious." She dropped to her knees and ran her fingers through her brother's hair. "We need to get him out of here."

"That will prove to be a problem." He eyed the shattered remains of the stagecoach and the dead horses. Then he turned his attention to Ilsa Smith. She had regained control of herself, but still clung to the squirming boy as though she'd never let go again. "Mrs. Smith, how are you faring?"

"I'm just fine, now, Mr. Brandish. I got my boy back."

"That you have."

Jane Weston stood and peered off into the distance, shielding her eyes from the glare of the sun off the shimmering land with the flat of her hand. "Oh, no, Captain Brandish! They're coming back!"

Brandish studied the rising dust cloud a minute and made a wry smile. "That's not the Apaches, Miss Weston."

"Not the Apaches? Then who?"

"That, ma'am, is the cavalry. A day late and a dollar short, as usual."

The column drew up, and the dust of their horses blew past the man at its head, who wore the bars of a captain on his shoulders. He surveyed the wreckage of the stagecoach, and the wounded. His gaze came to rest upon Brandish and narrowed a trifle at seeing the dusty blue of his uniform.

A man broke from the column and came forward, swinging off his horse. His hair caught the sunlight and shone like burnished copper. "Captain Brandish!" he said, clasping Ethan's hand.

"McGrath. You're a welcomed sight."

"We heard the shooting and came as fast as we could." McGrath suppressed a scowl and glanced over his shoulder. "Would have been here days ago but . . ." His eyebrow lifted and hitched toward the captain astride his horse.

"Brandish, is it? I've heard about you." The captain dismounted and looked about. "You've had some trouble with hostiles, I see."

"Some," Brandish replied, sizing up his counterpart. Captain Benton Ross was a shorter, leaner man than himself, and perhaps ten years his junior. He had the severe look of a man who took his job seriously.

"Are you hurt, Captain?" McGrath inquired.

"Not badly, but we have wounded." Brandish glanced at the column of soldiers, looking for the surgeon, Lieutenant Syrell. He spied him and ordered him over.

"You are in no position to give orders here," Ross snapped sharply.

Brandish stiffened. "Excuse me," he said, not attempting to hide his impatience. "In that case, you give the order."

The two men instantly disliked each other.

Ross said after a moment, "Mr. Syrell, please see to the wounded."

The surgeon came over, carrying a canvas bag of his medical supplies.

Aside, Sergeant McGrath said softly, "Would have started looking for you two days ago, but that high-and-mighty paper pusher from San Francisco had other notions."

Ross shouted orders for the column to deploy and secure the area. McGrath saw Jane Weston standing there and he smiled at her, tipping his hat a notch. "And how be ye, Miss?"

Jane did not return the smile, but seemed to stiffen some under his gaze. "I am fine," she said, edging closer to Brandish.

McGrath spied Ilsa Smith against the overturned coach and went to her. "And you, ma'am? Got yourself a wee bit o' an injury there I see. Well, don't you worry. We'll be getting you to the fort just as soon as we can. Syrell is a crackerjack surgeon."

"Thank you, Sergeant," Ilsa said.

While the doctor worked over Jonathan Weston, McGrath winked at Jamie, still clinging to his mother's skirts. "And what be your name, lad?"

"Jamie Smith, sir."

"That is Lieutenant Smith," Brandish said.

"Lieutenant Smith is it?" McGrath gave Brandish a grin.

"A field promotion for bravery in the face of the enemy," Brandish explained. He saw the scowl come to Benton Ross's face, but the cap-

Brandish

tain only looked away and continued directing the activities of his men.

"Who was the savage responsible for this?" McGrath asked.

"It was an Apache named Rock That Sparks. He won't be coming back today."

"What about Yellow Shirt? Have ye seen the renegade?"

"He's dead."

Jane shivered as the soldiers swarmed the area. She hugged herself and drew closer to Brandish.

"Dead is he?" McGrath glanced over to where Ross was deploying the soldiers. "That pompous willow twig had us out and about for days searching for Yellow Shirt. We crossed the trail of some Apaches on the way to Fort Bowie and that was all Ross needed. Looking for a feather to stick in his cap early on, he is. An eager beaver, that one."

Brandish grinned and said, "I seem to recall you saying something about seeing to it that he doesn't make any damned fool mistakes right off."

McGrath shrugged his meaty shoulders and frowned. "I can only do so much with the likes of Captain Benton Ross. God help the cavalry." He shook his head dejectedly.

Ross came over. "How long ago did the aborigines leave this area, and in which direction, Brandish? I don't want them to get away this time."

"Before you go running off after the Apaches,

shouldn't you send back to Fort Bowie for an ambulance to move these people?"

"You keep forgetting that you are no longer part of the cavalry, *Mr.* Brandish." He turned abruptly and began organizing a patrol to follow the Apaches' trail, and to report back to him. After he had that project moving to his satisfaction, Benton Ross ordered McGrath to assign riders to return to Fort Bowie for an ambulance.

"Would you like to go along to the fort?" McGrath asked Jane Weston. "I'm sorry I cannot offer you a proper saddle, but you are welcome to accompany us."

She stepped next to Brandish. "No thank you, Sergeant. I will remain here with Captain Brandish and my brother."

"As you wish, ma'am."

The ambulance arrived early the next morning. Jonathan Weston had regained consciousness, and Dr. Syrell was astonished that he had survived his ordeal at all.

"No doubt," Brandish told the doctor, "he comes from a strong lineage," and he found himself watching Jane drinking coffee by the morning campfire a few yards away. She looked over, caught his eye, smiled, and glanced away.

Ilsa Smith hobbled to the ambulance beneath the attentive care of Sergeant McGrath. "Thank you, Sergeant McGrath," she said as he turned her over to the orderlies, who helped her inside.

McGrath swept his hat from his head and said, "Me pleasure, ma'am."

Brandish

Brandish noted that Ilsa Smith had somehow changed, and he wondered if it wasn't just him that she had resented.

They broke camp, and Jane mounted the sidesaddle McGrath had brought back from Fort Bowie with the ambulance and extra medical help. She urged her mount near to Brandish.

Brandish helped Jamie aboard one of the McClellan saddles and adjusted the stirrups for him. Jamie had retrieved Brandish's saber earlier the previous evening from where the ex-captain had dropped it, and he seemed reluctant now to part with it. Brandish let the boy carry it with him.

McGrath rode up alongside Jamie. "Well, it seems our eager captain is off chasin' wild Indians just now. Since he has taken the lieutenant with him, and Mr. Brandish is retired, and Dr. Syrell is busy tending to your ma and Mr. Weston, that sort of makes you ranking officer, Lieutenant Smith."

"Me?"

"Yes, you. I'm waitin' for your orders, Lieutenant Smith. Do we get these troops a movin' on to Fort Bowie?"

Jamie beamed, clutching Brandish's saber as he rode to the head of the column with McGrath. The sergeant sang out and started them moving—with Lieutenant Smith's indulgence, of course. Brandish and Jane Weston fell in behind the ambulance, which had been placed in the middle of the column.

As they started north to Fort Bowie, Brandish peered one last time at the twisted remains of the stagecoach. Then he discovered he was looking at Jane Weston, and she was smiling at him.

Like Ilsa, something had changed in her, and he considered it a pleasant improvement over the frightened and troubled woman he had discovered only a few days earlier.

Chapter Twenty-five

Ethan Brandish was crossing the parade grounds on his way to the post stables when he spied Jamie Smith sitting on the porch with his knees drawn up and his back against the cool adobe wall. A trellis along the front of the porch, thick with ivy, and the wide overhang of the roof above, kept the morning glare and Arizona heat at bay. Brandish was passing the officers' quarters, and he knew the little house where Jamie and Ilsa Smith were staying belonged to a Second Lieutenant Dibbers and his Mexican wife, Rosy.

Brandish diverted his steps. Jamie glanced up. He'd been crying and now he quickly wiped his eyes and fixed a reluctant smile on his face. "Morning, Captain Brandish," he said.

"Morning, Jamie." Brandish took a dipper of

water from the clay olla hanging in the shade beneath the porch, drank deeply, and smacked his lips. "Nothing like a dipper of cool water. In these parts, Jamie, cold water is worth its weight in gold." He put the dipper back and said, "How's your mother doing?"

"The doctor says she's mending right good and that she might be up and walking in another week. Mrs. Dibbers is takin' real good care of her. She even lets Mamma sleep in her own feather bed. Mamma ain't never slept in a feather bed afore, she says. She wonders what the army is comin' to with such comforts."

"Pleased to hear the good report. Have you two decided where you'll go once she's well?"

"We're going back home," Jamie said at once. "Got stock to see to. Lieutenant Colonel Crook, he was real worried about our stock, 'specially once he learnt we had us a fine string of mules. He sent a patrol out just to see to the place till we get back."

"Did he, now? Well, I know as a fact that Crook is partial to mules, but I guess I never knew how deep it went."

Jamie grinned and nodded his head. "Mamma said she never heard of such a thing."

"Times change," Brandish said. "For the better, I hope. You watch over your mother, Jamie. You're the man of the house now."

"Someday I'm gonna be a soldier," the boy said proudly.

"You'll make a good one. Well, I need to find the lieutenant colonel before I leave."

Brandish

"He's out to the stables," Jamie said. "I saw him go on over earlier."

"So I have been informed."

Jamie eyed the saber leaning up against the adobe wall by his side. "I guess you'll be wantin' this back now that you're leavin'."

"Reckon so." Brandish paused thoughtfully, and then said, "You know, Jamie, where I'm going back East, I'm not sure what I would do with it. Got any ideas on that?"

Jamie shook his head. "No, sir."

Brandish pretended to consider the problem, even though he had already made up his mind a few days before. "Tell you what, Jamie, why don't you take care of it for me while I'm gone? I'll probably be back through these parts in a few years and I'll want to pick it up then."

"You mean you want me to keep it for you?"

"Just until I come through again. Would you mind very much?"

Jamie's face beamed. "Gosh, no! I don't mind at all! I'll keep it polished and oiled and it'll be just fine when you come for it!"

"Well, good. I feel better about it already. Now, you tell your mother good-bye for me, and take care of her."

"I will," Jamie said, his thoughts temporarily diverted from his grief.

Brandish left the boy there in the shade and found Crook in the stables, just as he had been told he would by Crook's orderly, who had informed him that the lieutenant colonel wanted to see him before he departed the fort.

Crook was dressed in his canvas stable-detail suit and was wearing a white cork helmet on his head. He was a trim and athletic man who looked younger than his forty-five years. His fierce blond forked beard was beginning to show streaks of gray, but Crook looked nonetheless a man who could march all day, fight Indians the next day, and spend the third joyously tramping up and down mountains hunting elk and grizzly bear— a sport he loved nearly as much as his other passion, the careful study of nature. It was this same sort of precise study that he gave to the Indians, and which had thrust him to the forefront of the Indian wars; an accomplishment even Sheridan had to grudgingly acknowledge.

"Ethan," Crook said, glancing away from the mules he'd been admiring beyond the rail where his tall boot rested.

"George," Brandish said, resting his arms on the top rail next to the lieutenant colonel.

"Beautiful animals, are they not?" Crook grinned, and added, "I'm speaking in the utilitarian sense, of course. They can carry more than a horse, on less food, and into more rugged terrain." He frowned then and changed the subject. "I hear you're about to leave."

"I figure it's time to go. There's no need for me to stay around here any longer. It only makes leaving that much more difficult. Your orderly told me you wanted to see me?"

Crook's blue-gray eyes were bright and sharp, like the cavalry saber Brandish had left in Jamie's charge. He said, "Yes, I did. Before you rode out,

Brandish

I thought I'd try one more time to make you change your mind. I can still get your commission reinstated. Heaven knows, I would rather have you out here with me than—" He cut his words short. It would have been unprofessional to berate a fellow officer. In spite of his eccentricities, Lieutenant Colonel George Crook was a consummate professional, even if at times an outspoken critic of the way some of the other commanders were treating the Indians. In many respects, Brandish and Crook were kindred spirits. The two men had recognized that long ago.

Brandish said, "I hear that Captain Ross has not yet returned from his patrol."

Crook turned away from the stall and the two man walked out into the harsh morning sunlight and across the parade grounds toward post headquarters. "I have to give the man credit. He doesn't let up. I have no doubt he'll catch up with that renegade."

"Like you, he subscribes to the Carleton-McDowell injunction."

Crook looked over and grinned. " 'Strike the trail while it's hot and stay on it at all costs until you have your enemy!"

"But he lacks your experience."

"Experience comes by doing ... and young Ross is doing. I knew his father during the war. I see a lot of him in Benton. They're both ambitious men"

"Is that good?"

Crook drew up and frowned at him. "Let's just say I'd rather it was still you back at Fort Lowell.

I understand you, Ethan. You were—are—a good officer." His frown lengthened. "And because I know you as well as I do, I understand why you feel compelled to leave."

Crook's words surprised Brandish. He wasn't certain if he understood his own motives himself. They continued across the parade grounds beneath the relentless sun glaring blindingly off of Crook's canvas suit and white cork pith helmet. Inside headquarters, Crook removed the hat and canvas coat and sat behind his desk. He motioned Brandish to a chair.

"What are your plans, Ethan?" he asked, and then quickly added, "Oh, I know, you told me already. You're going to go back East. That's a rather vague strategy for a man of your tactical caliber."

"I have no plans beyond that."

"You figure just to put some distance between yourself and this land with its injustices."

Brandish nodded his head thoughtfully. "Perhaps. I have plenty of time to decide."

Crook gave a short laugh. "No, my friend, you do not have plenty of time. Time is not on your side. It is not a friend, but an enemy. You're nearly my age, and although I try never to show it, I feel it. Deep in my bones when I wake in the morning, or after a long patrol running down these confounded Apaches. These last couple years have been hard."

"The troops wouldn't know it to look at you."

"Of course not. I've got an image to uphold." He laughed, then became serious again. "I know

Brandish

I can't talk you out of something once your mind is made up, Ethan. I knew that the moment I received your formal letter of resignation six months ago. Just the same, Ethan, I need you. Dammit, I need you on my side. But more than that, the Apaches need you."

Brandish studied Crook suspiciously. "What are you getting at?"

Crook picked up a brown envelope from his desk. "The day after I got your letter, I wrote one myself. I just received this reply. I was hoping the featherbrained politicians in Washington would make up their mind before you left the Territory."

There was a glint in Crook's eye. Brandish was curious. "What deviltry have you up your sleeve this time, George?"

Crook handed the envelope to him. "Go on, read it. It's from President Ulysses S. Grant."

"Grant?" Brandish extracted the letter and opened it. In a moment he looked over at Crook. "It's a transfer to the Department of the Interior, to the Bureau of Indian Affairs."

"I've acquired some pull after the campaigns of the last couple years," Crook said with a laugh. "The Bureau and I will never agree on policy. They don't want us soldiers running it, but the Eastern humanitarians they put in charge don't know their—" Crook paused and cleared his throat. "Well, I won't get into that. You know my feelings there. Let's just say they could use a lesson in general anatomy. But you see, Ethan, you're no longer in the military. You're a civilian now. You're honest and you have a sympathy for these people we're rounding up and placing in reservations. A man like you can do a lot of good in that job. Besides, I need a man in the Bureau that I can work with. You can help clean up the corruption. What do you say?"

Ethan Brandish was stunned by the offer, and for a long silent moment he sat there while Crook waited for his answer.

Brandish stopped by the post hospital before he left that morning. Jane Weston was in a chair at her brother's side when he strode in, his steps loud and hollow on the wooden floor. She rose immediately upon seeing him, and with a sudden, spontaneous smile, came across the room and took him by the arm.

"I was hoping you'd stop by before you left. Jonathan and I were just talking about you."

There was a new vitality in her eyes, and in her step, and right at the moment Ethan Brandish thought Jane Weston to be about the prettiest woman he'd ever laid eyes upon. He could not remember what it was about her that had made him decide she was plain that first day they met. He had already begun to question his recollection of that day, which although only a little over a week past, seemed more like a lifetime ago.

As she brought him to Jonathan's bedside, Brandish noted the marked improvement in the man lying there, and something else too that he did not immediately grasp. Then he understood. Jonathan had seen the change in his sister as well, and there was a look of relief in the man's haggard face, as if he knew that she had passed a turning point.

Jonathan reached out a hand, stifling a grimace. Brandish felt the returning strength in the man's grasp.

"I understand you're leaving." Strength had returned to his voice as well.

"Yes."

"Have you decided yet where you'll go?" Jane asked him.

"Back East, at least for a while."

"They say that California is a land of opportunity. A golden land." At once Jane colored at her boldness.

"Named after a mythical island of gold and jewels," Brandish added, smiling at her. "Someday, very likely, I will be in California. I'll be in touch with the Pacific Division frequently with my new job."

"You have a job?" Jane sounded surprised.

"It seems as though Crook couldn't let me leave in peace. He pulled some strings with President Grant and got me an appointment to the Bureau of Indian Affairs. For some reason, he thinks I might fit in there. I'll be returning to Washington for a while, and then it looks like I'm coming back here to the Territory." He grinned. "Crook is a man who gets things done. One of these days he'll make General."

Jane said, "Is it what you want?"

Brandish had to consider this a moment. After all, he had learned about the appointment less than an hour ago. "There's a lot of good I can do. The Apaches will not be able to hold out against the army and the crush of the westward expansion much longer, and they'll need all the help they can get to adjust to a new way of life."

Jane studied him a moment, a faint scowl showing. "You sound like you disapprove of progress."

He drew in a long breath, let it out, and said, "My personal feelings won't change what's meant to be. But perhaps working inside the system will. You asked me if this job was something I wanted. My answer to that is, yes."

"Then I'm happy for you, Captain Brandish—" She caught herself and smiled. "—I mean *Mr.* Brandish."

"I prefer the sound of *Ethan*," he said.

Her hand lingered upon his arm a moment longer than necessary. Brandish told Jonathan good-bye and Jane walked him to his waiting horse.

"I don't want to say good-bye, Ethan," she said as he tugged his hat back onto his head and buckled a holster belt around his waist. "I prefer to say, 'until we might meet again.' Take care of yourself, and . . ." She hesitated, her next words seeming to catch in her throat. ". . . thank you."

Brandish stepped into the stirrup and settled into the saddle. She appeared small standing there on the porch watching him. Small, but strong, and resolute, and Brandish knew she would do well in California. "When you get to where you're going, write me a letter in care of

Lieutenant Colonel Crook. I've got a feeling he'll always know where to find me."

"I will."

"Good-bye, Jane."

Brandish reined his horse around and rode away from the hospital. As he left Fort Bowie behind him, he regretted not being able to tell McGrath good-bye as well, but the sergeant was off with Benton Ross, still trying to chase down Rock That Sparks. He'd have to wait until his return to the Territory to see his old first sergeant again.

He descended into the baking oven of the San Simon Valley and his thoughts went back to that moment when Rock That Sparks and his small band of warriors had ridden away.

They would not be easy to chase down. That wily Apache war chief was going to give young Captain Benton Ross a run for his money, and Ross would soon discover that fighting Indians in the Territory of Arizona was a far different game than what he was used to at Division Headquarters back in San Francisco.

In fact, Brandish mused, Benton Ross might never catch that Apache! He was grinning as he rode out into that wide country that opened up before him.

DON'T MISS OTHER CLASSIC *LEISURE* WESTERNS!

McKendree by Douglas Hirt. The West had been good to Josh McKendree. He had built a new life for himself with a loving wife and a fine young son—but halfbreed trapper Jacques Ribalt took it all away from him when he slaughtered McKendree's family over a simple land dispute. Now, McKendree has only one thing left—a need to make Ribalt pay for what he did. And the West is just a place where his family's killer is hiding. And McKendree will see justice done...or die trying.

_4184-7 $3.99 US/$4.99 CAN

Mattie by Judy Alter. Young Mattie, poor and illegitimate, is introduced to an entirely new world when she is hired to care for the daughter of an influential doctor. By sheer grit and determination, she eventually becomes a doctor herself and sets up her practice amid the soddies and farmhouses of the Nebraska she knows and loves. During the years of her practice, Mattie's life is filled with battles won and lost, challenges met and opportunities passed.

_4156-1 $3.99 US/$4.99 CAN

Dorchester Publishing Co., Inc.
P.O. Box 6640
Wayne, PA 19087-8640

Please add $1.75 for shipping and handling for the first book and $.50 for each book thereafter. NY, NYC, and PA residents, please add appropriate sales tax. No cash, stamps, or C.O.D.s. All orders shipped within 6 weeks via postal service book rate. Canadian orders require $2.00 extra postage and must be paid in U.S. dollars through a U.S. banking facility.

Name_____
Address_____
City_____State_____Zip_____
I have enclosed $_____ in payment for the checked book(s).
Payment <u>must</u> accompany all orders. ❏ Please send a free catalog.

BACK TO MALACHI

ROBERT J. CONLEY
THREE-TIME SPUR
AWARD-WINNER

Charlie Black is a young half-breed caught between two worlds. He is drawn to the promise of the white man's wealth, but torn by his proud heritage as a Cherokee. Charlie's pretty young fiancée yearns for the respectability of a Christian marriage and baptized children. But Charlie can't forsake his two childhood friends, Mose and Henry Pathkiller, who live in the hills with an old full-blooded Indian named Malachi. When Mose runs afoul of the law, Charlie has to choose between the ways of his fiancée and those of his friends and forefathers. He has to choose between surrender and bloodshed.

__4277-0 $3.99 US/$4.99 CAN

Dorchester Publishing Co., Inc.
P.O. Box 6640
Wayne, PA 19087-8640

Please add $1.75 for shipping and handling for the first book and $.50 for each book thereafter. NY, NYC, and PA residents, please add appropriate sales tax. No cash, stamps, or C.O.D.s. All orders shipped within 6 weeks via postal service book rate. Canadian orders require $2.00 extra postage and must be paid in U.S. dollars through a U.S. banking facility.

Name_____
Address_____
City_____ State_____ Zip_____
I have enclosed $_____ in payment for the checked book(s).
Payment <u>must</u> accompany all orders. ❑ Please send a free catalog.

WILL HENRY

THE LAST WARPATH

"The most critically acclaimed Western writer of this or any other time!"
—Loren D. Estleman

The battle between the U.S. Cavalry and the wild-riding Cheyenne, lords of the North Prairie, rages across the Western plains for forty years. The white man demands peace or total war, and the Cheyenne will not pay the price of peace. Great leaders like Little Wolf and Dull Knife know their people are meant to range with the eagle and the wolf. The mighty Cheyenne will fight to be free until the last warrior has gone forever upon the last warpath.

**FIVE-TIME WINNER OF THE
GOLDEN SPUR AWARD**

___4314-9 $4.50 US/$5.50 CAN
**Dorchester Publishing Co., Inc.
P.O. Box 6640
Wayne, PA 19087-8640**

Please add $1.75 for shipping and handling for the first book and $.50 for each book thereafter. NY, NYC, and PA residents, please add appropriate sales tax. No cash, stamps, or C.O.D.s. All orders shipped within 6 weeks via postal service book rate. Canadian orders require $2.00 extra postage and must be paid in U.S. dollars through a U.S. banking facility.

Name_____
Address_____
City_____State_____Zip_____
I have enclosed $_____ in payment for the checked book(s).
Payment <u>must</u> accompany all orders. ❏ Please send a free catalog.

"Max Brand practices his art to something like perfection!" —*The New York Times*

MAX BRAND

THE DESERT PILOT/ VALLEY OF JEWELS

TWO WESTERN CLASSICS IN PAPERBACK FOR THE FIRST TIME!

The Desert Pilot. The town of Billman is known for its lawlessness, but Reverend Reginald Ingram arrives with high hopes to defeat the power of the saloons and gunsmoke. But soon the preacher may have to choose between his peaceful ways and survival.

And in the same volume...

Valley of Jewels. Beautiful Daggett Valley is pitted with danger. Here Buck Logan plots to con a half-witted old man into revealing where he has hidden a cache of jewels, but schemes don't always go according to plan, and before the end of the day, blood will be shed.

___4315-7 $4.99 US/$5.99 CAN

Dorchester Publishing Co., Inc.
P.O. Box 6640
Wayne, PA 19087-8640

Please add $1.75 for shipping and handling for the first book and $.50 for each book thereafter. NY, NYC, and PA residents, please add appropriate sales tax. No cash, stamps, or C.O.D.s. All orders shipped within 6 weeks via postal service book rate. Canadian orders require $2.00 extra postage and must be paid in U.S. dollars through a U.S. banking facility.

Name_____
Address_____
City_____State_____Zip_____
I have enclosed $_____ in payment for the checked book(s).
Payment <u>must</u> accompany all orders. ☐ Please send a free catalog.

ATTENTION WESTERN CUSTOMERS!

SPECIAL TOLL-FREE NUMBER
1-800-481-9191

*Call Monday through Friday
12 noon to 10 p.m.
Eastern Time
Get a free catalogue,
join the Western Book Club,
and order books using your
Visa, MasterCard,
or Discover®*

Leisure
Books